SELF STORAGE

Consolino Barsotti

SELF STORAGE

and Other Stories

MARY HELEN STEFANIAK

Minnesota Voices Project Number 80
New Rivers Press 1997

First Edition
Printed in the United States of America
Library of Congress Card Catalog Number: 97-68815
ISBN: 0-89823-183-3
Edited by C. W. Truesdale
Copyedited by James J. Cihlar
Book and cover design by Steven Canine
Set in Monotype Baskerville

New Rivers Press is a nonprofit literary press dedicated
to publishing the very best emerging writers in our
region, nation, and world.

The publication of *Self Storage* has been made possible
by generous grants from the Jerome Foundation; the
North Dakota Council on the Arts; the South Dakota
Arts Council; Target Stores, Dayton's, and Mervyn's
by the Dayton Hudson Foundation; and the James
R. Thorpe Foundation.

Additional support has been provided by the Elmer
L. and Eleanor J. Andersen Foundation, the Beim
Foundation, the General Mills Foundation, Liberty
State Bank, the McKnight Foundation, the Star
Tribune/Cowles Media Company, the Tennant
Company Foundation, and the contributing members
of New Rivers Press. New Rivers is a member
agency of United Arts.

New Rivers Press
420 North 5th Street, Suite 910
Minneapolis, MN 55401

www.mtn.org/~newrivpr

For John, Jeffrey, Elizabeth, and Lauren

day draws near

another one

do what you can.

CZESLAW MILOSZ
"On Angels"

CONTENTS

ACKNOWLEDGMENTS

My wholehearted thanks go to the Minnesota Voices Project and my astute and sympathetic editors at New Rivers Press, C. W. Truesdale and Jim Cihlar; to John Stefaniak and Judy Polumbaum, for careful reading and advice; to Jeff, Liz, and Lauren Stefaniak, for their patience and support; and to Sarah Lamb and Ellen Hickerson, for more than porridge.

I also wish to acknowledge the publications in which these stories first appeared: "Voyeurs" in *The North American Review* and the anthology *Bless Me Father* (Plume / Penguin / NAL, 1994); "America, the Beautiful" in *The Yale Review;* "The Lonely Seat" in *Short Story;* "Roof Raising" in *Agni;* "Self Storage" and "Stepping into the World of Men" in *The Iowa Review;* "On the Coast of Bohemia" in *The Source;* "The Dress from Bangladesh" in *Iowa Woman;* and "Dear Mike the Mechanic" in *The Crescent Review.*

Voyeurs

The first time Judy and I saw the naked man, it was by accident. We were thirteen, and we were crossing the Walnut Street
bridge over the railroad tracks, talking about whether we would
ever get an abortion or would we have the baby no matter what.
It was 1964. I said I would have the baby no matter what. So right
away Judy asked me if I'd seen the movie *The Cardinal,* which, I
knew, had been rated B by the Catholic Legion of Decency. It was
playing at the Avalon at the time. I reminded her that my mother
wouldn't let me see movies that were rated B by the Legion of
Decency. Well, said Judy (whose mother played the saxophone in a
three-piece band and didn't give a hoot for the Legion of Decency),
in the movie the Cardinal's sister gets pregnant. They all know it's
a risky business for her, but of course she goes ahead and has the
baby anyway—no matter what. "But then," Judy said, "in the middle of being born, the kid gets stuck somehow and the doctors say
the only way to save the Cardinal's sister is to crush the baby's head
and yank it out of her."

"Jeez, Judy," I said. "That's not *abortion.*"

Anyway, Judy told me, the Cardinal has to make the decision—
either save his sister's life by killing the baby or let them both die

naturally according to God's will. Years later, when I saw the movie on TV with my mother one Sunday afternoon, I remember I got so angry at her for being on the side of God and the Cardinal that I refused to stay for supper. Judy, however, didn't get a chance to tell me what the Cardinal decided because it was at that moment, as we reached the highest point of the bridge, that we saw the naked man.

He was in a fourth-floor window in one of the new brick apartment buildings next to the tracks. We decided later that he probably thought people on the street couldn't see him up on the fourth floor, but because of the little hill we were on and the hollow the building was in and the angle of the street and other fortunate features of the terrain, his window was a bit below our eye level and not more than ten or twelve yards from where we stood, rooted to the spot on the crest of the bridge.

Judy said, "Holy moly!" I said, "Oh my."

We could only see part of him—the important part—from below the shoulders to right above the knees. He had a lot of hair (red hair, like my accordion teacher Mr. Krumpf, I thought with alarm). It covered his chest and inched down his belly in a thick, curly triangle, diminishing to a copper-colored line that pointed—as Judy told Pam later—all the way to Texas. The naked man was thin (unlike Mr. Krumpf, I noted with relief). From the bridge we could see the shape of his ribs and hipbones. Of course, we were not much interested in ribs and hipbones. Judy took advantage of the opportunity to use one of her favorite words.

"Look at his cock," she whispered.

Judy and I had been best friends since first grade, but by the time we were thirteen, certain differences had developed between us, and "cock" was one of them. Judy teased me for saying "penis," a word she considered old-fashioned, anatomical, and lame. She would repeat it after me in a wheedly voice, drawing out the long "eeee" and the "ssss"—as in *sissy*—but I still couldn't bring myself to use her alternative. Not only because I believed that my mother would wash my mouth out with soap if she ever heard that I said it, but also because of all the other cocks I was afraid I'd ruin by association. Once I started using "cock" to mean *cock*, then what would I do in school, or in ordinary conversation—maybe with my mother!—when somebody said something was cockeyed? Cockeyed. Think about that. And what about stopcocks and peacocks and shuttlecocks?

Eleven-year-old Pam, who was the junior member of our best friendship, solved the problem by calling it a "thing"—which Judy said was better than "penis"—but I wasn't about to compromise "thing" either, and I had a cousin named Dick, so most of the time I tried to avoid calling it anything at all. Now, however, watching the naked man walk past the window with his penis/cock/thing swinging to and fro in full view, I knew I had to say something. I whispered vaguely, "You'd think it would get in your way."

"What?" Judy whispered back.

"You *know* what," I said. "Hanging down like that."

The naked man had stopped in front of the window. He was flexing his arm muscles, such as they were, this way and that, as if he were using the window as a mirror, while, down below, his penis adjusted itself to every change of posture.

"You probably get used to it after a while," Judy said.

We watched in silence for another moment—the naked man went on flexing and adjusting—and then the second worst possible thing that I could have imagined happening happened.

"Here comes a car!" I cried.

There was no place to hide on the top of the bridge. I would have run for it—foolishly calling attention to myself, Judy pointed out later—if she hadn't taken me by the arm and hauled me back to the railing, out of the path of the approaching headlights. There we leaned, with our backs to the tracks and the apartment building, just as if we had stopped to chat on the bridge, where—Judy also pointed out—we had every right to be at nine o'clock on a warm spring night. When the car passed—my heart was pounding so hard in my ears that I barely heard Judy say, "Coast is clear!"— we turned to look again. The naked man walked past the window wearing pants.

"Shoot," said Judy.

"Show's over," I said, my knees weak with relief.

We were both pretty quiet the rest of the way home. I was still trembling and thanking our lucky stars for what I considered a narrow escape. Judy—I found out when we reached my back porch—was thinking about something else. She sat down on the bottom step, avoiding the patches of light from the kitchen windows, and tossing her long, blond hair over her shoulder, she said into the night, "We could charge admission."

16

I sat down beside her. At a window behind us my cat appeared, casting a monstrous shadow at our feet.

"Admission for what?" I said warily.

"For the *show*," she said.

"What do you mean?"

"Hey—you're the one who said it," she said.

"What did I say?"

"'Show's over!'" she quoted me.

"Jeez, Judy, *that's* not what I meant."

She slapped me on the back and the cat shadow vanished. "So you're a genius and you don't even know it."

"But, Judy," I said, "what if we got caught?"

She stood up and started pacing in front of me. "Doing what?" she said. "Standing on the bridge? I mean, it's not like we used binoculars, is it? There's no law against standing on a bridge."

There were flaws in this reasoning, I was sure of it. Unfortunately, I didn't know what they were.

"But, Judy," I tried again, "what makes you think we'll ever see the guy naked again? Maybe he just forgot to pull his shade, you know?"

There was a moment of silence. Judy stopped pacing and sat down beside me again.

"Well?" I said, thinking my point had been well taken.

"Well," she said slowly. "Actually, I've seen him naked before."

"What?" I gasped. "Where?"

"What do you mean, where? In the window, of course. Same place, same *time*, same station—get it?" She leaned into me. "Look, kiddo. It's simple. All we have to do is blindfold people and lead them all around, through the bushes and over the tracks and everything, to the right spot at the right time! For a price," she hastened to add. "*Now* do you get it?"

"Judy," I asked her, "how many times have you seen this naked man?"

She tugged on her bangs. "Oh, once or twice." She fidgeted. "Well, actually, twice. Not counting tonight."

"And you never told me?" I was not only shocked but hurt. A naked man seemed like the sort of thing best friends should share.

Judy rolled her eyes. "I just *did* tell you," she said. "Now, are you with me or not?"

The next night we took Pam, who had five older brothers and knew about these things, to see the show free of charge. We stopped in the middle of the bridge, where Judy and I had been the night before, but I was so extremely nervous about waiting there, in full view of the occasional passing car, that we moved into the lilac bushes where they made a leafy cave at the end of the bridge and found that we could see the window even better from there. After about five minutes of swatting mosquitoes and thinking I heard footsteps coming over the bridge, I tried to make a case for going home.

"Come on," I whispered. "This guy isn't going to parade around in his birthday suit every night for our benefit. Let's go."

Judy and Pam ignored me.

"The mosquitoes are eating me alive," I said, slapping a big, bloody one on my arm and conspicuously failing to mention what was really bothering me. Last night, after all, I had seen the naked man more or less by accident, even if I did hang around and watch for a while. Tonight we had come looking for him. I was trying to think of a way to point out this fine ethical distinction to my friends when Judy grabbed both my arm and Pam's and said, "Look!"

Holding on to one another in the lilacs, we looked. There he was—same time, same place, and as naked as he'd been the night before.

"What do you think of *that?*" Judy asked Pam.

"You can see his thing, all right," Pam said. She turned to me in the darkness to see what I thought. Now was the time to share my reservations about window-peeping. Now or never. They both looked at me in the darkness. My two best friends.

"You can see it all right," I said.

18

The following night I found myself in the alley blindfolding
Carrie Tuttle, who'd risked her very life to sneak out of the house
after nine o'clock, and also Helen Mahoney, who'd come along
only because she happened to be spending the night at Carrie's
(and who was—I felt, knowing Helen—making a big mistake). Judy
did the same to Leah Fischer and Heather Wisniewski, while Pam
took care of the twins, Lenore and Linda. Then we led the six of
them, stumbling and giggling, around the block, through a couple
of yards, down over the railroad tracks, and back up to the spot.
When we took the blindfolds off, they were understandably annoyed
to find that they had paid a quarter each to be led to the end of
the Walnut Street bridge, and there was a lot of grumbling in the
lilac bushes for a while. To make matters worse, the naked man's
light was off.

"You see?" I whispered fiercely, taking Judy aside and leaving
Pam to ride herd on our dissatisfied customers, one of whom had
already scared me half to death by shrieking when a cricket landed
on her. "What did I tell you?" I hissed. "Just because a guy is naked
three nights in a row doesn't mean we can *count* on him—"

I stopped in mid-sentence. This time Judy didn't even have to
say "Look!" Her eyebrows told me to turn around. The light was
on in the window. Seconds later, our friend appeared from about
the neck down, shedding garments where he stood.

Everyone was impressed. Carrie and the twins agreed that the
guy's thing (I noticed they all said "thing") was easily the longest
one any of them had ever seen before (as if any of them had ever
seen one). Heather, an only child who always got the highest scores
in the class on her California Basics, admitted that this was the first
penis she had ever seen. "A handy thing to have on a picnic," she
mused. Leah Fischer wondered if red-haired men had freckles *everywhere* (we couldn't quite tell from the bridge), and poor Helen
Mahoney, whose glasses reflected the streetlight, giving her an
astonished, alien look, said nothing.

Nobody asked for her money back.

When, after a few minutes, the naked man disappeared from the
window, I had another quiet but heated argument with Judy about
whether or not it was time to go. Even she had to agree that the

nine of us made a pretty conspicuous crowd in the lilac bushes, and I think we might have left right then if the naked man hadn't chosen that moment to reappear with a towel thrown over his shoulder and, it soon became clear to us, something strange happening down below. I don't know what he was looking at or thinking about, but one minute his penis was hanging there, like always, and the next minute—

"Ho!" said Linda. "Look at that!" said Lenore.

"His cock looks like a diving board," Judy whispered, giving Pam an attack of giggles so severe that we practically had to suffocate her to keep her quiet. It didn't help matters that the others were giggling, too, all except for Helen, who would have been looking shamefacedly at her shoes if she could have seen them down there in the dark. By the time we had composed ourselves enough to look again, the penis was pointing straight up. It seemed to be trying to get a look at what it was attached to.

"*That's* an erection," Pam of the five brothers said authoritatively.

"It looks like a little person," whispered Heather, in something like awe.

The next night Judy had so many customers she had to take them in two shifts. She warned both new and returning ones—all of whom seemed willing to pay rather than venture to the spot on their own—that she couldn't *guarantee* what they would see on any one night and that they might have to spend more than a quarter to get their money's worth. For several nights in a row, she and Pam had the lilac bushes filled to capacity. Each of those nights, Judy reported, the naked man obliged them by turning on his light, right on schedule, although his fantasy life, from all appearances, seemed to be in something of a slump.

I didn't go back to the bridge again. I told Judy it was because my cat had run away, which was true. She had. She was a clawless indoor cat unacquainted with the dangers of traffic, and for days after she disappeared I approached with dread all crumpled bags and piles of leaves or garbage in the street. I even examined a freshly flattened squirrel to make sure it wasn't a cat. I spent my evenings on the back porch waiting, hoping, with milk and tuna fish, and Judy helped me post my Lost Cat signs everywhere, but Nancydrew never came back.

In the meantime, the end of May turned into the beginning of June, the lilacs faded, and I couldn't believe, as more and more girls found out about Judy's little operation, that nobody had blown the whistle on her yet. When she told me that she and Pam were thinking about extending their word-of-mouth advertising to the public junior high, I told her she was nuts.

"You don't even know those kids," I said. "What if one of them turns out to be a wimp and tells her mother?"

"Helen Mahoney didn't tell," Judy countered. "Who could be more of a wimp than Helen Mahoney?"

I had the feeling it was not a rhetorical question.

The first week of June was also the last week of school, when, according to tradition, a priest took the eighth-grade boys into one room and a nun took the girls into another for a last-minute session in sex education. I don't know what the priest told the boys, but Sister Lucinda was not too explicit. She showed us a couple of pictures— cross-sections of pertinent male and female anatomy—briefly discussing the "deposit" of sperm in a prim, precise way that made me think of bank tellers and pneumatic tubes, and then she went straight to the Ninth Commandment, where she lingered for some time.

Thou shalt not covet thy neighbor's wife covered a great deal more territory than it spelled out, she emphasized. It covered impure thoughts, dirty magazines, B-rated movies, and more, she said, as she looked with knowing eyes from one of us to the next. I remember glancing at Judy to see if she was taking this in. She met my eye for only a second, but it was long enough to tell me that she didn't need Sister Lucinda's list of sins any more than I did. We both knew what the commandment covered; it covered the naked man.

Later, I clutched Judy's arm. "She knows!" I said.

"Oh, she does not."

By this time I realized that Judy and Pam were going to be in big trouble sooner or later if I didn't do something to stop them. Unable to convince them of the danger they were in, I wracked my brain for a way to eliminate what Sister Lucinda would have called the occasion of sin. Somehow, for the sake of my friends (and, I believed, for decency's sake as well), I had to get the naked man himself to close the show.

There seemed to be no safe way to contact him. I didn't know his apartment number (there were sixteen all together, I learned from checking the mailboxes of an identical building on Locust Street), and I was not going to throw a rock through his window or otherwise seek him out face to face. For one whole catless, friendless evening I pondered. Then I thought of writing the notes.

I used the nice pink notecards with matching envelopes that Aunt Cecelia gave me for my birthday every year. After fiddling with the wording for a long time, I settled on this:

> Dear Sir,
> People can see you naked from the street.
> Please pull your shade or something.
>   Signed,
>   A concerned neighbor

Needless to say, I omitted the return address. I also took the precaution of riding my bike down to the post office instead of using the box at the end of our block to mail the pile of pink envelopes, each addressed to the "Occupant" of a different apartment number from one to sixteen.

When I told Judy what I'd done, she was furious. She said I had no business ruining everything for everybody else. She said why don't I go hang around with Helen Mahoney then. She said the Ninth Commandment was about coveting your neighbor's *wife*, for God's sake, and they weren't coveting anybody anyway. They were only looking at him.

"But, Judy," I tried to defend myself, "how would you feel if he was looking at you?"

Judy narrowed her eyes at me. To this day I remember the way she narrowed her eyes at me. She said, "Whose side are you on, anyway?"

America,
the Beautiful

Staramajka told me, "Georgie my boy, better to eat food cooked in the gutter, than under the same roof where people shit."

She said it in Croatian. On principle she never learned to speak English. She pretended all her life that she didn't understand a word.

"Tch," said my mother, who sat at the table between my grandmother and me. "Baka, this is not your little Novo Selo, this is Milwaukee in Wisconsin of America." She waved her hand at the view from the kitchen window, past the next block of houses and the car barns and the tracks and the grain elevator, past the drop forge where my father worked second shift, to the river. "It is not the Drava River out there. It is the Kin-Kinni-"

"Kinnickinnic," I said. "It's an Indian word. It means tobacco made from the bark of trees."

Staramajka glared at me. She had very few teeth, and when she worked her jaw in anger her face collapsed.

"I learned at school," I said in my defense, and I returned my attention to the bowl of hot cereal in front of me.

"I am telling you," my grandmother began again, "better to eat food cooked from the gutter—"

"Tch!" My mother stood up abruptly and whisked away my cream of wheat. I heard the bowl clatter in the sink. Staramajka stood up slowly, her lower lip jutting over the upper, reaching almost to her nose, and she padded scornfully out of the kitchen on bare feet gnarled like the roots of a tree.

24

"She does not live in the United States of America," my mother said after her, and it was true. America was like a painful dream for my grandmother—our upstairs flat, the Serbs who lived downstairs (thirteen of them, including nine children and one old old man who played chess in his underwear all day), the noisy street, the nearby factories, the drop forge that regularly sent her hand to her heart and the color draining from her face. America was some nasty trick of the atmosphere that hid from her sight the cottages and the muddy cowpath and Father Klima's stone church with the grave of my grandfather behind it. She never accepted their loss. She made *kolaci* and streudel for neighbor ladies five thousand miles away, and pretended not to notice when we ate them instead. When one of the rich women my sister ironed linens for gave us a radio, Staramajka sat for hours beside it in the front room, carrying on animated conversations in Croatian with the Voice of Firestone. One day my mother asked her, "Why do you talk to the radio, Baka? It cannot hear what you say." My grandmother smiled up at her bitterly, toothlessly, from her seat beside the Zenith. "Who is there who can hear what I say?" she said.

I was the one who saw the ad in the paper and read it to my mother and my grandmother at breakfast that morning:

Now, at SEARS and ROEBUCK!
A New Modern Bathroom Can Be YOURS!
Pure White Porcelain Commode
White Enameled Tub
And Standing Sink!
Just $55.95 COMPLETE!
Easy payment plan available

"What is 'Commode'?" asked my mother.

"I think it means the toilet," I said in Croatian, and that's when my grandmother entered the discussion.

For of all things that Staramajka found barbarous about America, the worst—the foulest, most uncivilized, and blasphemously unclean—was the custom of having indoors, under the same roof where you lived and slept and cooked your meals and ate them, a toilet. (Having never lived anywhere else but in her tiny village, she believed this to be an exclusively American arrangement.) A toilet within spitting distance of the stove was how she put it, with a little shiver of disgust. At first, she was lucky. Our flat did not have a toilet—not under the same roof anyway. We had to go downstairs and out the back door and turn to the left into a little room built on the side porch, which the five of us (my mother and father, my sister Magdalena, Staramajka, and me) shared with the thirteen Serbs. This indoor-outdoor *kupatilo* had a sink and a bathtub and a toilet that flushed weakly if you filled the bowl from a bucket that we kept in the tub. In the winter, a bath was life-threatening. In the morning, there was always a line.

Not long after I found the ad for the enameled tub and the porcelain commode, my mother rose before daylight, as she always did, to make breakfast for my father before he left for his first-shift railroad job. She hurried downstairs to visit the bathroom while the oven heated up, never thinking to knock on the door at such an hour, and found our Serbian chess player naked in the tub with his chessboard set up on the toilet seat. Though he was visible only by the glow of his cigar, my mother saw enough. That very afternoon, we took the streetcar to the Gold Coast on the upper east side, where my sister worked, and transferred, the four of us, to the Mitchell Street line. We were on our way to Sears.

I could see right away that the salesman did not like the look of us—three generations of babushkaed women (one with no teeth to speak of) and me, a skinny, shifty-eyed boy. We had agreed on the streetcar that Magdalena would speak for us. She had hardly been to school here and her English was much poorer than mine (she had a talent for making it more broken or less, as the situation required), but my sister had presence. She was taller than our bespectacled salesman and not in the least shy about bathrooms or anything else in the world. She gave him a dark-eyed smile to melt any heart.

"We look for the bathrooms," she said.

The salesman raised a delicate eyebrow, pronouncing each word as though he had selected it carefully and still it left a bad taste in his mouth. "The ladies' room is located in Carpets and Appliances, next to the luncheonette."

"No, no. This one. In the paper." Magdalena held out the folded newspaper and tapped the ad with her finger, smiling.

"Bathrooms to buy," my mother put in.

My grandmother scowled.

"You wish to buy?" the salesman said, lifting his voice in musical disbelief.

He led us through a maze of nickel plate and porcelain to a little platform covered with green felt, where a gleaming toilet, a pedestal sink, and a bathtub with the claws of an eagle stood like statues on an altar. My mother and sister hurried forward with little exclamations of pleasure to touch the smooth porcelain and shining fixtures. I would have followed them—I wondered if there was water in the toilet—but my grandmother pinched my elbow just then in such a way that I felt it to my fingertips. She pulled me back behind a plumbing display into the next aisle. When I turned to look at her, her jaw was working and her eyes glowed.

"What is it, Staramajka?" I glanced around to see if there was anyone to hear me talking like a foreigner.

"Now *I* wish to see the bathroom," she said.

"We were just looking at it." I tried to turn back to the green felt platform.

"No, no. I mean the one in Carpets"—she grimaced—"near the restaurant."

"I thought you didn't understand English, Baka."

"You will take me there, now, to the room for ladies."

"You mean the ladies' room."

"*Ladies.* Tch." She took me by the sleeve.

We found our way by asking a clerk and then just following our noses.

"Jesus, Maria," my grandmother said. "What a stink!"

The corridor that led from the carpet department to the ladies' room was barricaded by a large Out of Order sign; behind it, a man in work pants that were wet up to his knees pushed an enormous rag mop, trying to swab up the water that covered the floor in the little corridor and crept out to darken the patterns of several display rugs. Two fellows in double-breasted suits who were, apparently, the Carpet and Appliance salesmen had stationed themselves in the out-reaches of their respective departments, as far as possible from the ladies' room, and still their nostrils flared.

"Let's get out of here," I said, breathing through my mouth.

But Staramajka stood her ground on a damp Persian rug. She seemed excited by the scene. She followed with her bright eyes the movements of the man with the mop, watching him heave it into a bucket and squeeze it through the wringer, then slap it back down on the floor again.

"Is the water from toilets?" she said to me.

"How should I know?" I wanted to get clear of the smell.

"Ask him. Ask him." She gave me a little push.

"What do you care?"

"Ask."

I asked. It was. She looked delighted and repelled at the same time. By now the fellow with the mop was frowning at us.

"The ladies' room is closed," he said. "For repair." His face said we must be pretty stupid if we couldn't see that for ourselves.

Staramajka snorted. She looked right at him and said—though of course he couldn't understand—"You are up to your ankles in water from toilets."

This was an exaggeration, but I think her tone of voice made him even more uncomfortable than his wet shoes and pants. He stood his mop up like a staff in front of him, holding it with two hands. "You can use the men's if you want." He pointed to our right, to a door marked GENTLEMEN on the border between Damp Carpets and Appliances.

"Hvala," my grandmother said, "but no."

The man went back to his swabbing, and I touched my grandmother's arm, but she shook me off. Her face contracted in a frown of deep concentration as she watched the fellow wring out his mop.

"Esscooz," she said. "Vhy eez mess?"

I stared at her. Maybe my mouth fell open.

"Huh?" said the workman.

"Vahter comes on floor?" she said. "How?"

It was birds, he said. In cold weather, birds perched in the warmth on the edge of the soil stack, where it was vented on the roof. They couldn't perch there for long before they were overcome by fumes (I could believe that) and passed out and fell head first into the pipe. You get enough birds in there over the winter to clog it up, and instead of escaping out the roof the sewer gas builds up. Eventually, it escapes the only way it can. Bloop.

"That's what smells so great," he said.

Staramajka kept nodding and nodding at him all the while he spoke. When he was finished, she said, "Vhat kinda birds?"

I gasped.

"Starlings mostly," the workman said. "Once in a while sparrows, but they're so small they can find other cracks to keep warm in. Or maybe they're just smarter than them shithead starlings. Ha!" He looked from my grandmother to me. "You get it? I said them birds are shitheads!" He slapped his knee in appreciation of his joke and laughed the louder, and Staramajka looked from him to the mop to the pools of water on the floor and began to chuckle herself, her cheeks wheezing in and out. I felt the stares of the Carpet and Appliance salesmen.

"C'mon, Baka." I tugged on her elbow and whispered urgently in her ear. *"Hajdemo!"*

"Da, let's go," she repeated.

On our way back to Bathroom Fixtures, where my mother was putting her seven dollars down and signing away six dollars a month, I turned on my grandmother.

"You speak English, Baka," I accused her.

She gave me her best blank but good-natured look. *"Ne,"* she said, shaking her head. *"Ne govorim engleski."*

*　　*　　*

A week later, when the men from Sears came to deliver the toilet, my grandmother answered the door. It had long been her job to dispose of bill collectors and other undesirables by nodding and smiling, and smiling and nodding, while they explained their business, then shaking her head and repeating, *"Ne razumem. Ne govorim engleski. Ne, ne. Ne razumem,"* to their increasingly frantic gestures until, at last, she closed the door, gently, in their faces.

My grandmother was home alone when the Sears truck stopped in front of our house. The deliverymen stood on the upper landing outside our door for a while, pleading with her at first, sweating and finally cursing, before they carried the big wooden box marked Fragile back down the stairs. I got home from school in time to see the delivery truck pull away from the curb, with two of the littler Serbs perched on its rear bumper. They rode down to the corner with grins on their faces.

When my mother found out from the same little Serbs that her bathroom had come and gone, she got very excited.

"Baka!" she cried when she got back from Solapek's, where she had used the phone. "Why did you not tell me they already have come with the toilet?"

My grandmother stood at the kitchen table, up to her elbows in flour, squeezing fry-cake dough. (She baked and cooked from morning till dark those days, against the time when she would no longer be able to do so—under the same roof.) I was helping her, making rings of the dough, poking my thumb through the middle of each ring, and lining them up on the floured cloth. I could see in my mother's face her losing battle to control her temper. My grandmother said, without looking up, "It must have slipped my mind."

"Oh? Yes? Perhaps it is your mind that slipped!"

"No doubt you are right, Agnes." Staramajka patted the mottled dough in her hand as she would pat a baby's bottom. "I am an old woman," she added apologetically.

"You!" my mother cried. "You are, you are—" Words failed her. Overcome by anger and guilt—having shouted at her husband's mother—she rushed from the room.

"Tch," my grandmother said.

For three days, while I stayed home from school on my mother's orders to await the second coming of the toilet, tub, and sink, my grandmother hardly spoke to me. When they finally came to transform the pantry into the *kupatilo*, Staramajka sat on the upstairs porch the whole time. And the following day, when a plumber came to extend the old pipes and the soil stack and hook everything up, she shut herself up in the front room and assailed the radio with her grief.

She devoted the weeks that followed to showing that, when it came to shitting and eating under one roof, she was right and we were wrong. She took an interest in Mr. Slutzky's pigeons that only I understood. When she thought no one was looking, she sprinkled corn meal or flour in the rain gutters around the upstairs porch and tossed handfuls from there to the roof. I don't know if she was planning well ahead, or if she didn't realize that there was very little chance, in May, of stuffing the soil stack with cold pigeons.

She ate all her meals, even drank her coffee, on the upstairs porch—hauled her kitchen chair and an orange crate out there for good, overriding our pleas and objections. What if it rained? She'd wait until it stopped. What about wintertime—the cold and the snow? She said nothing, but I knew she had plans for cold weather. I'm sure she thought one good toilet disaster from the hand of God—via His birds of the air—would convince us once and for all of the perversity of having a toilet where the pantry should be.

By early summer she consented to cooking in the kitchen on the days my mother worked, even though she herself would not eat there. (The toilet was off-limits to the rest of us while she cooked.) After a month of lonely meals out on the porch, she must have wanted to eat with us again, but she simply could not. More than a year would pass—although, eventually, she moved inside to the front room—before she could sit down to eat in the kitchen. "But imagine, Georgie," she would say to me out on the porch when once in a while I joined her there, "imagine eating in the outhouse!" To her, it was all the same.

She found it convenient, when she cooked, to show her contempt for the bathroom by flushing kitchen garbage down the toilet. My mother told her not to, told her that coffee grounds and potato peelings did not belong in the toilet. If my mother had realized how much damage could be done, I think she would have asked my father to speak to Staramajka, but a second-story toilet was a new thing for all of us, and my mother's objections to using it as a garbage disposal came more from her sense of delicacy than from any practical concern for the plumbing. Of course, it was exactly my mother's sense of delicacy that my grandmother wanted to violate. And so the weeks passed, with Staramajka taking her meals on the porch, and the pipes taking a beating.

*   *   *

My own part in the story of my grandmother and the toilet might have ended there had it not been for Loretta Adams, who sat two rows over and one desk up from mine in the seventh grade at St. Augustine's that fall. Loretta wore her hair in red-gold braids and she had freckles not only on her nose and cheeks but down her chubby arms and—I once saw when she leaned over the Communion rail—across her chest. More important, she had breasts. They pressed impatiently against her little-girl clothes. She spoke English with an all-American lisp, and I was deeply in love with her.

It's not easy to be twelve years old and in love, even without the ethnic barrier I felt existed between me and Loretta Adams. (How could I bring blond and pink Loretta home to thirteen Serbs and a grandmother with no teeth who spoke Croatian to the radio?) In class, I watched her sucking on the end of her braid as she read the movie magazines hidden inside her speller. In the school yard, I watched her fling her leg over the back fender of Kevin Harding's bicycle for the ride home, her freckled arms wrapped around his waist. Before long, it was Otto Bernstein's bicycle and blissful smile I had to envy. Then Emil Swoboda's. Finally, it became clear to me that what I needed to win Loretta's heart was not an American name or ancestry. What I needed was a bicycle.

And I knew where I could get one. Frankie Tomasic had one for sale. He'd found it in the dump—we all scoured the dump daily but the windfalls always seemed to go to Frankie—and he'd fixed it up and refused to lend it to me because he knew I had the money to buy it.

It was the money I had been saving for my grandmother's teeth. I have said that she was toothless, but this was not entirely true. She had two top teeth and three bottom teeth remaining in the front of her mouth. They were not enough to keep her, when she scowled or laughed or even smiled, from looking more witchlike than grandmotherly. Small children sometimes ran away at her approach, and

I knew the Serbs downstairs told tales about her. Besides all that, we had studied in geography about the Plains Indians, among whom loss of teeth meant death by starvation. Certainly my grandmother was skinny enough. Back in the days when she ate with us in the kitchen, I would sit across from her and stare as she pressed and mashed and ground her gums together, chewing and chewing her noodles and bread and boiled cabbage. When I saw a sign in the window of the Modern Systems Dentist's office that I passed by on my way home from school, I determined to buy dentures for Staramajka. The sign said:

GUARANTEED HOLLYWOOD PLATE
ALL PINK, UNBREAKABLE PEARL TEETH
$65 Value: $27.50!
FAMOUS WAFER PLATE, $25 Value: $12.50
Good Rubber Set $5.50
10-year written guarantee with all work
FREE Extraction of Teeth on Better Plates!

Not knowing much about dentures, I thought I would surprise her with them—wrap them up in a fancy box and set it on her nightstand, or maybe next to her plate at dinner one Sunday. I started to save the nickels, dimes, and quarters I earned by selling carp and snapping turtles we caught in the river, or sacks of grain that we gathered from "emptied" railroad cars down by the grain elevator, or copper wire that we stole from Milwaukee Standard Wire and Tube.

I had nine dollars and seventy-eight cents saved up when I talked to Frankie. "I was thinking of asking ten," he said. "It's worth fifteen, easy, but—since you're my friend—I could let you have it for, oh, say, nine dollars and seventy-five cents." Not much taller than I was, though four years older, he stood in the school yard with his hand on the black leather seat in such a way as to cover the hole he had patched with electrical tape. I felt the terrible injustice of it all—Frankie's smirk, my grandmother's gums—and I considered telling Frankie to go to hell. But there was the bike, with its remaining spokes sparkling and a passenger seat mounted over the rear fender. And there was Loretta, flinging her leg over the rear fender of someone else's bicycle every day after school. I handed over the money, feeling the loss with each *clink* into Frankie's grimy palm.

By the time I got the bike home, I'd figured out how to ride it. I came, wobbling a little, around the corner, and the moment I saw her up there on the porch in her kitchen chair, chewing and chewing on something and frowning hard at the boy on the bicycle who was coming down the sidewalk, I was filled with remorse. For nearly a year I had been planning her teeth! When I looked up again, she was standing, her hands clasped in applause, grinning down at me, forgetting herself in her excitement. I felt even worse.

"Agnes! Agnes!" she called to the door behind her. "Look at your son! Magdalena! Come see your brother!"

I hauled the bicycle up a whole flight of stairs to the porch and the three of them surrounded me, exclaiming over the bike, delighted to learn it was mine. My mother forgave me the river filth I brought home on my clothes when I went fishing (she didn't know about the stolen grain and copper), and my sister asked if she could ride it. But my grandmother was the most excited of all. She stroked my hair and the fender alternately and said I looked like the young man who brought the mail to the postmaster in Novo Selo—such a nice young man, he would ride with a packet of letters in one hand, doffing his cap with the other, and he never once fell, not even on that dirt road full of ruts and holes and cattle droppings. She'd always thought he had his eye on her sister's youngest girl— but then he was killed in the war, she supposed, like the rest of them. She didn't know for sure, of course, because they had dragged her off to America, but most of them were killed. Such a nice *mladić*. By the time she finished talking, tears dripped down onto the bib of her apron.

Every day when I rode home from school she was waiting and watching on the porch. Every day she stood up and waved as I rounded the corner and smiled down at me over the railing as I got off the bike. If I waved my homework at her, she leaned so rapturously over the railing that I feared for her safety. It wasn't too hard to convince myself that I gave her more joy with the bicycle than she ever would have gotten from the teeth.

*   *   *

At school, I would take the little key I wore around my neck (on a cord Staramajka had braided for me), and I would put it in the padlock and draw the iron chain carefully through the spokes, all without so much as glancing in the direction of Loretta Adams as she climbed up behind Emil Swoboda and rode off clinging to him, her skirts whipping around their legs. I just bided my time and parked my bike in the rack next to his. Mine was the only one with a real passenger seat in the back.

"Nice bike," Loretta said one day, at last, as I unlocked it. She was waiting for Emil to come out of the building.

My face flashed red. "Thanks," I said coolly and rode off, pedaling hard.

Not long after that, Emil Swoboda stayed home from school one day, sick. When I came out of the building, Loretta was waiting for me. She had her hand on the seat of my bicycle.

I wasn't used to the extra weight and almost dumped us into the packed dirt of the school yard, but Loretta only giggled in my ear and squeezed me tighter around the middle. I hardly breathed for the whole ride home. If my mind had been working, I would have changed my route to avoid my house on the way to hers, but it wasn't (not with Loretta's front against my back), so I didn't. Staramajka was on the porch, as usual, as I came around the corner. When she saw Loretta—who was shrieking "Wheeeeeee" as we came down the hill and sticking her legs out straight to either side ("To keep from getting her feet caught in the spokes, Staramajka," I argued later)—my grandmother stood up and went inside, banging the door behind her. When I got back from Loretta's, she was waiting.

"So, who is this *kurvica* who is riding you home? Ha? Who is she?" She worked her lips over her gums while she waited for an answer, sucking them in and pressing them together. I thought about the Hollywood Plate.

"She's—her name is Loretta."

"Her *name*," Staramajka said, waving her half-eaten chunk of bread in my face. "Who *is* she, I want to know. Where did you find her?"

"She's in my class at school."

"In your class? That *kurva*—"

"Baka!"

"—is in the class seven that *you* are in? Hunh!" She made a loud blowing noise of disbelief, the lower half of her face ballooning in and out. "Look at me right in the eye, Georgie."

I did.

"This little hussy is in your grade at St. Augustineschool?"

"That's right, Baka. But she's not a hussy."

My grandmother, who believed in the evil eye and the pinch of salt thrown over the shoulder to ward off disaster, also believed that you could not lie with your tongue if your eyes said the truth. She relented, her face crumpling, except for one raised eyebrow. "So," she said, "how many times must she flunk to be in the grade seven, huh?"

"She never did," I said, although Loretta Adams had come new, and fully developed, to St. Augustine this year. I remembered the sweet soft squeeze of her behind me on the bike and I wondered.

Not that it mattered. From then on, out of sheer stubbornness, I made a point of bringing Loretta down my street every afternoon. My grandmother made a point of being on the porch just until we came around the corner so I could see her get up in a huff and go inside. Still, I was not prepared for the day that Loretta announced, as we came around the corner and bore down the hill, that she had to go to the bathroom.

"We'll be at your house in a minute," I said, pedaling faster.

"But yours is right here," she said as we flew past it. "Georgie, I really have to go."

Oh, I knew afterward that I should have ignored the urgency in her voice. I should have let her pee on my rear fender if necessary, but instead I took her around the block and back to the flat. There was no Staramajka on the upstairs porch, not even the first time we went by, so I began to hope against hope that maybe she wasn't home. At the same time I worried about where she would have gone. I decided to risk leaving the bike in the lower hall—in spite of the usual gang of little Serbs hanging around—in the interest of getting Loretta in and out as quickly as possible.

Upstairs, I opened the door and poked my head into the front room—nobody—and into the kitchen, while Loretta stood a little uncertainly in the doorway. There was no one in the kitchen either, but it looked as if Staramajka had left in a hurry in the middle of cleaning two big fish, bullheads by the look of them. They were stretched out side by side on her cutting board, headless, with the wooden handle of a knife sticking out of the belly of one of them. I rolled up a heap of entrails in the newspaper she had spread on the table and dropped the whole mess on the tiny platform of our back porch.

"Staramajka?" I called softly out the back door and down into the yard, thinking she might have come this way to avoid us.

"George?" I heard Loretta calling from the other room. I hurried back, pausing to wipe my bloody hands on the tablecloth my grandmother had folded neatly over a chair.

Loretta stood by the piano in the front room, with one knee resting on the bench, running her fingers noiselessly over the keys. She looked suitably impressed by it—an enormous oak upright that had come with the flat because somebody had brought it up through the front windows years ago and then changed the front windows in such a way that the piano wouldn't go back out again. It was a story my mother loved to relate, as if the free piano had been a piece of her own cleverness. None of us really knew how to play, although my father, who played the fiddle, could pick out a tune by ear. "Is this a player piano, Georgie?"

I admitted that it was. I wondered why my grandmother would run out in the middle of cleaning fish. She must have seen us coming—that was the only explanation.

"Ooh, can we play it then? Are the rolls in here?" and she lifted the lid of the piano bench.

Unless she had been taken ill, I thought. "Listen," I said to Loretta, "I thought you said you had to go to the bathroom."

"I *do*," she said. She looked indignant, her lower lip protruding ever so slightly, ever so petulantly, in a subtle copy—it struck me speechless, I remember—of the way Staramajka wrapped her lower lip over her upper. That's how it would look, I thought, staring, if she had *teeth*.

Loretta dropped the lid of the piano bench. "Where *is* the bathroom?" she said.

"Here. There, through the kitchen." I made a move as if to lead the way.

"I can find it just fine myself, thank you," said Loretta. She marched through the doorway and hesitated, sniffing. "Ugh," she said. "Fish." Her voice grew fainter as she made the turn into the bathroom. "I could smell it all the way in the other roo—"

She ended her sentence in the middle of a syllable, there followed two or three seconds of absolute silence, and then somebody screamed.

I leaped to my feet from the piano bench at the same moment that Loretta appeared, white faced, in the kitchen doorway. "Loretta?" I said, running to her. "Loretta?" She was so pale that I thought she might faint, but when I reached for her she went red in the face—red all over—and hit me hard, in the chest, with both fists. "Loretta!" I wheezed. She was pounding down the front hall stairs before I even caught my breath.

I made my way to the bathroom and paused in the doorway. Puddles of water filled the depressions of the floor, some spilling into the kitchen. But surely, I was thinking as I stepped carefully around the puddles, a leaking toilet, a little water on the floor, was not *so* terrifying, when a little noise behind me made me stop. I spun around.

Poor Staramajka was behind the bathroom door, her hands to her heart and a look on her face—well, a look that might have made *me* scream if I hadn't known the heart behind it.

"Baka?" I said. She pointed without a word to the toilet.

I looked, gasped, jumped back. Staring at me, glassy-eyed, from the toilet bowl—its whiskers waving—was the biggest bullhead I had ever seen.

"Jesus, Maria," I said.

"The fish, the fish," Staramajka moaned behind me. "He is stuck."

"Oh, Baka," I said, for I could picture my poor grandmother bending over the toilet to flush that fish head good-bye. I could see her face as she watched the water swirling around the opaque eyes and gaping mouth, whirling the fish to life for a terrible moment, and then rising, rising up to the seat and over it, spilling onto the floor and still running, flooding. The water swirling around her shoes. And then, on top of it all, Loretta. Oh, Staramajka, I thought, how sorry I am for everything.

She came up behind me, put a trembling hand on my shoulder, and peered over it at the fish, which stared back at both of us. "I have broken the toilet?" she said.

"Maybe not. Maybe we can just, uh, unclog it."

She watched me pull the fish head out—I had goose bumps all over, putting my hand in there and taking hold of its whiskers— and we both stood back to give the toilet a trial flush. Staramajka sighed as the water gurgled down with its sound like an old man clearing his throat. I turned to her, my heart full of things I had no words for.

She, too, looked thoughtful. She wrapped her lower lip over the upper and shook her head. Then, for the first time in many weeks, she put her arm around me. I waited for her to speak.

"Never flush a fish, Georgie," she said at last, with another sigh. "The guts go down. But the heads get stuck."

The Lonely Seat

As soon as we turned onto our street, the moment we caught sight of the mailbox on the corner and, a little farther down, the ragged top of the dying elm that threatens our garage, we knew that something was different, that things were not the way they used to be. "Did they cut down another tree or something?" my son Eric asked from the backseat. Meredith, my wife, thought maybe the streetlight in the middle of the block was new. We couldn't decide.

It wasn't long before we found out what was different. Meredith and I were still checking closets and under beds, making sure no intruders had set up housekeeping while we were on vacation, when the doorbell rang. The white-haired woman who lives across the street stood on our porch. "Oh," she said to me, "such terrible news."

Meredith, who had come up behind me, said, "What is it, Mrs. Strub? What happened?"

The neighbor pressed her hands together. "Curtis Gordon drowned," she said. "Little Curtis."

Somebody had drowned. "Who?" I said. Meredith gave me a sharp look and elbowed me out of the doorway. "How did it happen?" she said. "When?"

It had happened right after we left, the neighbor told us. Curtis Gordon had been fishing with some other boys down below the power plant, when he stepped into a hole and just like that he was gone, swept downriver.

"Oh, how terrible," said Meredith. "His poor mother."

Our white-haired neighbor shook her head. Two days after the tragedy occurred, she told us, his mother was still coming out on their back porch after dark, calling Curtis to come in. She leaned a little closer and added, "They'd already found the body by then."

"That poor woman," said Meredith.

I was still going up and down the street in my mind, from house to house. Which one was the Gordons'? "What about the father?" I asked, hoping for a clue.

"He called the doctor for her," the neighbor said. "Can't blame him. He was afraid she might hurt herself." She paused. "Curtis was an only child, you know."

"Those poor people," Meredith said when the neighbor left. Through the living room window we could see that she had stopped in the side yard to talk to our children, all three of whom were standing near the frog house Eric had made last summer out of wood scraps and window screen. They listened solemnly to her and stared down into the roofless box at their feet when she had gone. After a while, Eric stooped down and lifted something out of it.

"I suppose I should go see her," Meredith said suddenly.

I turned away from the window. "Who?"

"Rose Gordon. Curtis's mother."

"Why?" I asked her. I had figured out at last which house was the Gordons'. It was the one with the magnificent two-level tree house in the yard, four or five doors down from us, on the other side of the street we called the Great Divide—a three-lane current of one-way traffic, most of it hot off the freeway and all of it coming right at you if you chased a ball into the street or darted out from between parked cars. For years we had almost made a point, for safety's sake, of not getting to know the people who lived on the other side. I couldn't imagine going to see the Gordons now. I couldn't even picture their son's face. "What would you say to them, Meredith?"

She stared past me out the window. The children were gone now, the frog house roof replaced crookedly. "I'll tell them how sorry I am, that's all."

Within the hour, Meredith had gone across the street. I stayed home and wandered around the house, putting things away and watching from the window as the children made preparations— picking flowers, fooling with different-sized boxes they had piled up beside the frog house—for what could only be an ill-timed frog funeral. When I finally came out to ask them what was up, they showed me the withered remains.

"He must have been hiding," Eric said. "Otherwise I would have put him back in the creek with the rest of them before we left." He stood up beside his sisters and the three of them considered the deceased with regret. "Frogs don't always know what's good for them," said Jenny.

Reluctantly, I followed them to the burial ground in the back yard, under the lilac hedge. Digging the hole, Eric was careful to avoid the upended bricks, popsicle stick crosses, and softball trophy that marked the graves of other frogs, fish, birds, lizards, and a baby squirrel we tried to rescue after it had fallen from its nest. My daughters stood by respectfully, the unfortunate frog lying in repose in a shoe box at their feet, and I surveyed the debris of summer in our yard.

A rain-spotted aquarium half-buried among the hollyhocks caught my eye. The tadpole tank. I wondered what it was doing out here in the hollyhocks. We had found it in the basement the day we moved into the house, and Eric filled it immediately with pond water and bluegills from a park nearby. The fish died overnight, occasioning grief and the softball trophy in memoriam; but the water, we soon discovered, was alive with tadpoles—tiny tadpoles that looked like commas, hundreds of them sweeping through the green water in a single, tireless figure eight. We kept them in the tank until their tails shrank and their limb buds grew into legs and, one by one, they joined the ranks of tiny frogs—hardly bigger than houseflies—who looked surprised to find themselves floating on sticks on the surface of the water. Eric used to spend hours lying on the grass, watching them. Was it four years ago? He was eight then. Jenny was five.

Once, through an open window, I overheard her ask him why the little frogs just sat there like that. Why didn't they hop away? He told her they were resting. "Metamorphosis is hard on frogs," he said.

Under the lilacs, Jenny lowered the shoe box into the fresh grave, and Leah, our youngest, tossed a bunch of zinnias in after it. Dusting off her hands, she looked up at me and said, "Somebody drowned."

"It was Curtis, from across the street," Jenny added.

"Dad already *knows*," Eric said. The way he said it reminded me of the time he announced at dinner that somebody's dog had to be put to sleep. After a moment's silence, Leah had asked, "Is he still sleeping?" and Eric had snapped at her, "No, stupid, he's *dead*."

"Well," said Jenny, obviously offended, "you know what else? I figured out what's different about our street."

"What?" I asked, wondering all of a sudden how Meredith was doing over there.

Jenny lifted her chin and tossed her blond hair over her shoulder before she said, "The Gordons took their tree house down."

*   *   *

The children were still putting the finishing touches on the frog's grave when Meredith returned from across the street, looking puzzled. Rose Gordon, she reported, hadn't seemed crazed with grief at all. She had thanked Meredith for coming and expressed regret that our sons hadn't gotten to know each other better, since they would have been attending the same junior high in September. "That's what she said." Meredith frowned. "They would have been." Strangest of all, Meredith said, Rose had offered to give our son a ride to school every day. "She says it's on her way to work."

"What did you say to that?" I asked, and Meredith looked at me, surprised.

"I said no thanks. What do you think?"

On the first day of school, Meredith was still upstairs drying her hair when Eric left for the bus stop. I was in the kitchen with the girls, rattling through the dish rack in search of spoons. All at once, the whir of the hair dryer overhead stopped. We heard Meredith shouting to me, "John! Quick! Stop him!" I ran to the hallway and found her in her slip at the top of the stairs. She was pointing out the window, aiming the hair dryer like a gun. "Eric just got into that car!" she cried.

A silver station wagon was pulling away from the curb in front of our house. I made it outside in time to see the car turn the corner, two doors down. Eric, who was in the front seat, happened to look back at that moment and saw me leaning over the porch railing. He waved to me. I waved back. Then I went into the house, feeling a little foolish.

Meredith was waiting for me in the front hall, a robe thrown over her slip and her hair blown all wild around her head. "You could have run after them," she said.

"Meredith," I said, "he waved to me. It was somebody he knew."

"It was Rose Gordon," Meredith said.

"Well, sure!" I said. "She must have been on her way to work, like she said, and when she saw Eric—"

"She was waiting for him."

"What do you mean, waiting for him?" I noticed that Jenny and Leah were very quiet at the kitchen table, listening. I lowered my voice. "You don't actually think she was sitting in her driveway, across the street, watching our front door?"

Meredith did not lower her voice. "I think that's exactly what she was doing." She tugged on the ends of the belt that wasn't quite keeping her robe closed. "After I *told* her."

That afternoon, Meredith left work early to pick Eric up at school.

"What is this, anyway?" he asked me as soon as I got home. "Mother's Transit or what? In case nobody noticed, I'm not in kindergarten."

Meredith called immediately from the kitchen, "Did you tell *her* that this morning?"

My son—who is the image of his mother, from his blue eyes to his long legs—raised his eyebrows at me, shrugged, and followed me into the kitchen. "But, Mom," he said. "She just gave me a ride to school. What's so terrible about that?"

"You don't *need* a ride to school." Meredith pulled a pizza from the freezer and slapped it on the counter.

"I know, but she was right there. She pulled up right next to me."

With her back to us, Meredith stuck the tip of a knife under the plastic wrapper and ripped it off the pizza. Then she turned around. "What did you say to her?"

"What do you mean?"

"On the way to school—did you sit there in silence all the way like you did on the way home? What did you talk about with her?"

"I don't know."

"What?"

I gave my wife a surprised look that she ignored. Eric thought a moment. "Ballet," he said.

"Ballet?" Meredith and I said together.

"Yeah. I told her about the tickets Mom got from work. They're for the ballet, right? I told her you were making us go to every show because we had free tickets. She said she and Mr. Gordon go to all that kind of stuff."

"Great," said Meredith.

"She said Curtis never liked to go along either. She kind of laughed when she said that. I thought that was a little weird." Eric looked at us to see what we thought.

"Then what?" Meredith asked.

"Nothing."

"What do you mean, nothing? You couldn't have gotten to school that fast."

"No, but we really didn't say anything else, I don't think. Until I got out of the car."

"What did you say then?"

Eric put on a surprised and self-righteous look. "I said *Thank you.* For the ride. What do you think?" When Meredith didn't respond, he took a walnut from the basket on the table and examined it carefully. "And I guess I told her I was sorry about Curtis, about what happened to him, even if we weren't good friends. Curtis and me, I mean."

Meredith, who had bent to put the pizza into the oven, straightened up. She said, in a small voice, "What did she say to that?"

"She just said, 'You're welcome, Eric.'" He hesitated. "'See you tomorrow.'"

As soon as we'd finished the pizza and the children had left the room, Meredith called up Rose Gordon and told her, briefly and firmly, that while it was kind of her to give Eric a ride this morning, he really preferred to take the bus with the other kids. Sitting at the kitchen table, I could hear, intermittently, a high-pitched tremolo at the other end of the line. Meredith frowned at the phone for at least a minute after she'd hung up. Then I said, "What other kids?" and she frowned at me instead.

*   *   *

The year that Curtis Gordon died was also the year that we took turns sitting in the lonely seat. Meredith had won our season tickets for the Performing Arts Center in a drawing at the company picnic in June. "Four seats for six matinees of quality family entertainment!" was the way her boss, as master of ceremonies, described the prize. When Leah heard that, she did a little quick arithmetic involving the fingers of no more than one hand and ended up tugging on the boss's sleeve as he flipped hamburgers at a row of Weber grills. "How come I don't get to go?" she asked him. "I'm six years old." The following Monday, Meredith received a fifth ticket by interoffice mail for a seat that was in the same section as the other four, but ten rows down, right on the aisle. "Who has to sit in the lonely seat?" Leah asked then, and Meredith told her, "We'll take turns."

The single seat turned out to be the best of the five. Not only on the aisle, but in the very first row of the balcony, it offered its occupant the luxury of resting arms and chin on the railing, with no danger of somebody coming along to spoil the panoramic view. When the season opened in September with the Budapest Folk Dance Ensemble, we drew straws to see who sat where, although my son offered to save us the trouble by spending the afternoon at the video arcade. He was the one—"the lucky duck," according to Jenny— who ended up in Leah's lonely seat.

Meredith saw very little of the Budapest dancers. She was too busy craning her neck to see over and around the crowd, making sure that our son was still there at the edge of the balcony. Once, when the house lights came up, she thought she saw the Gordons in an expensive box off to the left. It was the third seat, empty, beside them—more than the man's height and baldness or the woman's reddish hair—that gave her the idea they were the Gordons. She had already nudged me, pointing discreetly, when the couple stood up and revealed themselves to be somebody else.

The next month, when Jenny drew the short straw for a mime troupe from Marseilles, Meredith's view of the single seat was blocked by tall people in the intervening rows. She nearly drove me crazy that afternoon, elbowing me every few minutes and saying, "Can you see her? Is she still there?"

"Where else would she be?" I kept whispering back, trying to ignore the sighs and fidgeting going on behind me whenever I sat up very straight and dutifully spotted my daughter's head, ten rows down in the dark and haloed by the lights on stage, a reassuring pair of braids outlined in gold above the lonely seat.

*   *   *

It soon became clear to me that Meredith was watching the Gordons, their comings and goings. "He's cutting the grass," she would say to me on the porch, or, if she saw Rose get out of the car cradling grocery bags, "She went shopping." It was as if their continued existence right across the street never ceased to amaze her. Sometimes she posted herself at the window in the front room when Eric left for school in the morning—just in case—but Rose Gordon must have changed her schedule, Meredith reported, for there was never any silver station wagon in the drive at that hour.

One October afternoon I came home early, took the newspaper out to the front porch, and finished half the front section before I happened to look up and see all three of my children in the Gordons' driveway across the street. I'd thought they were at the park. I was surprised—not horrified, the way I imagined Meredith would be—but at least surprised. They were shooting baskets.

I paged through the paper a little longer, and when I looked up again, Mr. Gordon was out there with them, giving them pointers. I watched him stand beside Jenny, hunching down to her height, his hands over hers, and show her how to use her wrists, how to bend her knees a little. Then he showed them how to sink one from across the court, and he let Leah put her hand over his while he dribbled the ball all around the driveway. I could hear her giggling from where I sat.

Later, I watched them cross the street to come back, Eric holding Leah's hand and touching Jenny's arm to keep them on the curb until the cars passed. They all looked left and right and left again before they ran across together. When they reached the porch, they barreled up the steps right past me, shouting, "Time for 'Star Trek'!" instead of hello. I stayed outside for a while and watched Mr. Gordon shoot baskets by himself. He was pretty good. Suddenly our front door opened and Eric stuck his head outside.

47

"Hey, Dad, we couldn't put a tree house in that old tree, could we?" With his thumb he indicated the elm, already leafless, over the garage.

"Heavens, no," I said. "Just look at it. It wouldn't be safe."

"I *told* Jen," he said, and disappeared again.

A few minutes later, I heard the crunch of tires on gravel as Meredith pulled into our driveway. She saw me on the porch and came over to kiss me hello. "He's out there playing basketball," she said. Maybe I should have told her then about the children playing with him, but I didn't. I said, "You know, we'd have to pave the driveway to put a hoop on our garage."

*   *   *

When the For Sale sign appeared on the Gordons' lawn, Meredith said, "They're moving!" Soon there were other signs—their trash cans stood at the curb with broken chairs, wood scraps, an old stroller, piles of magazines. Curtains disappeared from some of their windows. The Purple Heart truck picked up boxes and bags from the doorstep. And on a Saturday morning, early in November, while Meredith was grocery shopping and the children watched cartoons upstairs, Rose Gordon came to our door, carrying a very large cardboard box. I knew immediately that it was Rose Gordon, although we'd never met, by her red hair, which is visible from across the street, and by her eyes, which were wide-open green and always on the move, as if she were expecting something to appear just outside her field of vision at any moment and felt continually surprised that it hadn't shown up yet. She was gripping the box so tightly that its lower front corners were caving in. She smiled at me over the top of it.

"You must be Mr. Meyer," she said, shifting the weight.

"John," I said. Her cardboard box smelled musty, as if it had spent time in slightly damp storage.

"John," she said. "I'm Rose Gordon. From across the street." Then she laughed. "We meet at last," she said. "After four years of being neighbors!"

I said something about the busy street, the danger for children darting across—then stopped in confusion.

"It *is* a dangerous street," Rose agreed, still smiling. With a barely audible grunt, she set the box down and straightened up again, brushing her palms together. "I've brought over a few things I thought the children might like," she said. There was something proprietary about the way she said "the children" that made me wonder how much time they spent across the street when Meredith and I weren't home. "Really," she said, "some of these things are like new. There's a denim jacket, especially, that we had custom-made. Gorgeous needlework on the back. I'm sure it would fit your boy."

I looked down at the box at my feet. The caved-in cardboard claimed to contain four dozen jars of baby food but held instead clothes that had belonged to Rose Gordon's son, clothes custom-made for the boy who had drowned. I shuddered to think what Meredith would say if she found these things on our front porch, much less on her son's back. "Thank you," I said to Rose, "this is very nice of you but—"

"Oh, you're welcome, you're welcome," she said, looking around and sweeping invisible dust from her sweater. I thought her gaze came to rest on the three bicycles leaning against the outside of the porch railing. Her eyes lost a little of their alertness, looking at the bikes. She said, "We're moving at the end of the month."

"Yes," I said, grateful for something harmless to talk about. "We saw the sign. Where are you going?"

"Florida," she said, apparently to the bicycles. Then she looked at me. "Howard got transferred to the Jacksonville office."

Now it was my turn to say something. Rose Gordon kept looking at the bikes—I was not imagining that—and in the silence they seemed to loom larger and larger beside the porch. I continued to fail to think of something to say. The silence grew. It expanded to suffocating proportions, as if silence were rising like a fog from the floorboards. I was afraid that if one of us didn't speak up soon, I would find myself apologizing to this woman for having three living children—children who rode bicycles, who did not die, who went fishing but did not drown. I had actually taken a breath to begin, when Rose Gordon saved me.

"I have to be going," she said briskly. "Take what you want and give the rest to Goodwill." She turned and hurried down the steps to the sidewalk, leaving me and my apologies on the porch. At the curb she stopped and called back to me, "Don't throw them away." Her smile was gone, and I noticed that she didn't look before she crossed the street.

I carried the box inside—it was damper and mustier in my arms—and left it in the living room while I went to the kitchen. I had already decided to put the clothes in a garbage bag and take them directly to Goodwill, even though what I suddenly wanted to do was to go through the box and find that not a single item in it resembled anything my son had ever worn. The important thing was to get it out of the house before Meredith got home. I was snapping a plastic bag out of the cupboard when I heard the front door open. I stopped, and then I heard my son's voice.

"Holy shit—I mean, geez, Mom, look at *this*."

From the kitchen, down through the hall, I could see both of them in the living room—Meredith hugging a grocery bag and Eric kneeling on the floor beside the box of clothes, opened now. He was holding up the denim jacket, showing his mother the back of it.

"That's really . . . something," I heard Meredith say.

For a moment, neither of them saw me hesitating between the kitchen and the dining room. Eric stood up and slipped his arms into the jacket. Now I could see the back of it, too. Embroidered in metallic thread, an eagle spread its wings from armhole to armhole. "Isn't this *great?*" Eric said. He headed for the mirror in the hall and saw me standing in the doorway, garbage bag in hand. "Dad," he said, "check out this jacket." He stuffed his hands into the pockets and craned his neck to see the golden eagle on his back.

To my surprise, watching him in the jacket made my throat feel dry. "Where did it come from?" he asked.

I said, "Mrs. Gordon brought it over. It belonged to Curtis."

The silence in the living room was so complete that Meredith— still out of my sight but within hearing—must have been holding her breath. I don't know what I expected my son to do when I told him about the jacket—tear it off with a shiver of horror and throw it back into the box?—but he only looked at me blankly for a moment. Then he said, "How come she gave it to us?"

Meredith stepped into view at that moment, squeezing the hell out of her grocery bag. "Take it off, Eric," she said.

"But, Mom—"

"Take it off."

"But it's a great jacket."

"Take it off."

"But she *gave* it to me."

"Take it off and put it back in the box."

Still he hesitated.

"Before I take it off for you."

"Oh, all right!" He shrugged out of the jacket and let it fall to the floor. "You don't have to make such a big *deal*," he said, giving the box a shove with his foot.

Only after we heard the front door slam behind him did Meredith sink down beside the box and start stuffing the jacket and other escaped items back into it. "Why is she doing this?" she kept saying. "What is she trying to do? I'm going to take this box right back across the street and ask her—"

"Meredith," I said.

She went on punching the jacket with the eagle, which looked as if it were trying to get back into the box where it belonged. "I'm going to ask her right out—what are you trying to *do?*"

"Meredith."

All at once she stopped punching and looked up at me. "They're *damp,* John," she said.

"I know." I stooped down. She watched me slide the whole box into my garbage bag.

"They're full of *mildew,*" she said, and her eyes filled with tears.

*   *   *

Rose left the fishing poles on the porch. It was maybe a week after she had brought the clothes over. Meredith opened the front door in the morning and three of the poles—two very nice rod-and-reels and a serviceable bamboo—clattered to the floor across her path. Tight-lipped, she headed for the phone.

That evening, Howard Gordon came over to apologize for his wife's behavior. He sat in our living room, hands on his knees, one or the other of his long fingers twitching. "I talked to her about it," he told Meredith and me. "I said, 'How do you know these people want these things?' She said, 'Why wouldn't they want them? They're perfectly good fishing poles. Expensive ones.' I said, 'But maybe they already have good fishing poles.' She said, 'No, they don't.' I said, 'How do you know?' She said, 'The children told me.'"

Meredith sat up very straight. I looked out the window.

"I'll talk to Rose again," Mr. Gordon promised as he stood up to go. "But she—it's hard to explain—she seems to think, by giving these things away, she's honoring the memory of our son. Sort of"—here his voice got hoarse—"spreading him around." He looked down at his hands—big hands that could easily palm a basketball—and for a terrible moment I was afraid that he was going to cry, but he looked up again, dry-eyed. "We'll be out of here before Christmas," he said.

As soon as he was out the door, Meredith turned on me. "You *knew?*"

"Well, sure, they've been over there a few times after school."

"You *let* them go across the street?"

"I didn't exactly let them. They just went. Eric is twelve years old, Meredith. You can't tell a twelve-year-old kid he's too young to cross the street."

"But the girls—"

"The girls only went if he went. I made sure of that."

"So you *did* let them go. And you never told me."

Meredith had this wild and desperate look, as if she were surrounded by conspirators on every side. Determined to be reasonable, I said, "Think about it, Meredith. Do you really think we should deny that poor woman"—I left the father out of it—"whatever small consolation she gets from our kids? If you were Rose Gordon, wouldn't you need all the consolation you could get?"

Meredith's eyes went hard. "If I were Rose Gordon," she said, "I'd jump off a bridge."

*   *   *

Sometime between the delivery of the clothes and the discovery of the fishing poles, Meredith shared one of her nightmares with me. Not that she told me about it. She never told me about them. She'd wake up crying somebody's name—usually Eric's or mine, though once it was Curtis Gordon's—and she'd claim she didn't remember a thing in the morning. She communicated this particular dream to me directly, I'm sure of it, while we slept, through the contact of her leg over mine, or the curve of her back curled against me.

In the dream I was watching tadpoles with Eric, who was very small, maybe two years old, maybe three. He said, "Hold me up, Daddy. Wanna see." As soon as I held him over the tank, though, he began to shrink. He shrank so fast that he slipped through my fingers. I was afraid to grab for him, he was so small, so small and falling, I was afraid I'd crush him snatching him out of the air. So I let him fall into the water—that seemed the safest thing to do. The tank was small, I'd find him easily. But every time I scooped up a handful of the murky green water, there were only tadpoles in my hand, tadpoles or tiny frogs that hopped away as fast as I caught them. Finally, in anguish, I looked into the tank and saw Eric in the bottom, under the remaining water, still shrinking and crying "Daddy!" until he disappeared.

*   *   *

A moving van pulled into the Gordons' driveway on December 4, a Friday, and stayed there for two days. Mr. Gordon supervised the first day of loading, but after that we saw no more of him or Rose or their silver station wagon.

"They've gone," Meredith said.

We had tickets to see *The Nutcracker* on Sunday, and instead of drawing straws we had decided to let Jen and Leah share the single seat for this one, changing places at intermission. Leah was thrilled at having her turn at last. "It works out just *perfect*," she said. But on Saturday, both Eric and Meredith came down suddenly and violently ill with the flu. And on Sunday, as curtain time approached, Meredith, who could hardly lift her feverish head off the pillow, started dropping hints about the Gordons, and whether they were really gone, and she begged me not to let either of the girls sit all alone now that there was no need. Wanting to soothe her, I put a cool washcloth on her forehead and promised to keep both girls with me. I stopped in Eric's room, too, and told him I was sorry he had to miss the ballet. "I'll live," he groaned.

In the car, the girls were furious with me. "You mean we're going to *waste* the lonely seat?" Jenny asked.

"Give me a break," I said. "A promise is a promise."

"But you promised me first," Leah wailed.

"That's true. You did," Jenny said. They worked on me all the way downtown, knowing, I think, that my resistance was low after a mostly sleepless night of delivering aspirin and glasses of water. Whatever the reason, in the end, the promise I chose to break was the one I made to Meredith. She would forgive me, I reasoned, when her head was clearer.

The theater was packed—mostly with children in holiday clothes, running ahead of their parents in the lobby and bouncing on the red velvet seats inside. I had a moment of misgiving as I watched Leah strut down the aisle alone, her coat over her arm. She looked back over her shoulder at us only once, with a grin of sheer I-can't-believe-I'm-getting-to-do-this delight. "Just till intermission," Jenny called after her.

I fell asleep almost as soon as the house lights dimmed. When I awoke, seconds later, the curtain was going down, the lights were coming up, and Jenny was shaking my knee. "Where's Leah?" she was saying. I looked down the rows to the single seat. It was empty.

My first ridiculous thought was that she had fallen over the railing. We ran down the balcony aisle—against the current of the crowd surging toward the lobby for intermission—and looked over the edge, but there were only coats and programs scattered on the seats below. No broken bodies. I ran back up the aisle, dragging

Jenny after me, to the lobby, where we stood for a moment, buffeted by waves and eddies of children, their parents stationed like watchful towers among them. I must have spotted Leah a half-dozen times at least, but she always turned out to be somebody else in a red-and-white dress.

I tried to think of what to do next. Should I call the police? Notify security? Tell them to lock all the doors before the kidnapper got away? I thought of the unbearable absurdity of dialing my own number and informing Meredith that our daughter was gone. I had lost her. And then what? After the police and the futile search and questioning, would I have to go home with one daughter instead of two? My chest tightened. I thought of Rose Gordon standing on my front porch with her cardboard box and her vigilant eyes. I gripped Jenny's hand so hard that she said, "Ouch!" and then, "Look."

She pointed into the crowd. In the midst of the red and green and ruffled children, an usher stood, tall and official in her blue uniform, flashlight and programs tucked under one arm and at the end of the other, holding her hand, was Leah. For a second, I didn't believe it—I'd been fooled before—but then Leah saw us and let go of the hand and came running, dodging other children, explaining loudly as she came that she had to go to the bathroom and I was sleeping, so Lisa took her. Lisa the usher smiled. Jenny rolled her eyes. I thought: A reprieve. Justice or no justice.

I sat through the second half with Leah on one side of me and Jenny, very sullen, on the other, but I still couldn't shake the panic I'd felt at first sight of that red velvet seat—empty. I'd look down and see it again, and a burst of adrenaline would shoot straight through me to my fingers and toes. You couldn't keep them safe, I thought. You had to keep them safe, but you couldn't.

After the ballet, I drove home slowly, coming to a complete stop at every stop sign and looking right and left and right again before I proceeded. I asked the girls, "Are you buckled?" and then, when we crossed the river, I imagined the bridge collapsing under us, my daughters securely seat-belted to their doom. It was no use. You couldn't keep them safe. My knuckles were white on the steering wheel when we turned our corner and passed the Gordons' house.

The moving van was gone. The last load of trash waited at the curb.

"There's our fishing poles," Leah said sadly as we drove by.

I pulled into our driveway and turned around in my seat to ask her, "What did you say?"

"The fishing poles." She pointed across the street. Two fancy rods and the bamboo stuck up out of a green garbage can.

55

We got out of the car. "Wait here," I told them.

I went to the curb, looked both ways, and crossed the street, wondering all the while what in the world I would tell Meredith about this. When I reached the row of garbage cans, I stopped. It wasn't easy to pull Curtis Gordon's fishing poles from the trash. I had to shake off a tangle of line and a styrofoam cup stuck to the end of one of them before I got them out. When they were free, I laid them across my palms, testing their weight. I held them steady while their long ends sprang and danced, and balancing them, like a tightrope walker, I crossed the street again.

Roof Raising

Hattie Blount had stopped grieving for her husband long ago, but she couldn't seem to stop waiting for him. No matter how busy she kept herself during the day, no matter if she never even thought about him once all day long, she was still waiting underneath, quietly, waiting the whole time until it got to be nine or ten o'clock—which was the time he would have come home one night thirty-two years ago if his Pontiac hadn't met up with a pickup truck. Only then, at nine or ten o'clock, when she was standing in the front doorway, with the light behind her throwing her shadow down the porch steps to meet the larger darkness—only then would she realize that she'd been waiting for the day to be over, and now it was over, and there was nothing left for her to do but go to bed.

That was why she liked going fishing in the morning. When she was fishing, all Hattie needed was a tug on the line and her loose ends and unnamed longings came together: she knew that tug was exactly what she'd been sitting there waiting for. True, there wasn't much in the way of fish in the branch of the Ocmulgee that ran behind her property—not like in the old days when she and Pete could catch breakfast in half an hour if they got up early enough, back when their three scrubby acres were way out beyond the edge of town, not a single office park or subdivision in sight, nothing out here but the old Arctic Circle Drive-in on Jeffersonville Road, Home of the Best BBQ in Central Georgia, and the very place that Pete was heading home from in his Pontiac, with his brother Ed and Eddie's wife Frances and a one-quart carry-out that the sheriff found, leaking but intact, under the front seat. The Arctic Circle was a parking lot now, and sometimes the whole morning passed without a nibble on Hattie's line, but she didn't mind. At least she knew exactly what was missing.

Caroline, the niece that Hattie had raised like a daughter, did not understand. She sat on the stoop of Hattie's cottage, a crazy quilt of lean-tos and add-ons behind the real house—the big, empty stucco house—and told her aunt that it was a waste of time to sit by the river all morning the way she did, getting bitten up by horseflies and mosquitoes.

"Bugs don't bite me much," Hattie said. "I used to have to slather you and Ronnie up with baking soda, but not me. Your Uncle Pete used to say—"

"What about rattlesnakes, Aunt Hattie? What about water moccasins?" Caroline would say these things while Hattie was getting her fishing gear together. She would say them with a sidelong glance at little Lizbeth, who might be playing with the worms in Hattie's bait bucket.

"You know there's no moccasins come this far downriver, Caroline. Not anymore."

"No fish either."

Caroline was still snappish on account of the house. Fifteen years ago, Hattie had tried to give the place to her niece, as a bribe, to keep her from moving to God knows where with her Air Force husband. Hattie even mailed her a photocopy of the deed on their honeymoon in the Poconos, all ready for Caroline's signature, but Caroline never so much as mailed it back unsigned. That was long ago, before Hattie got it into her head that she couldn't talk Caroline out of leaving, any more than she'd been able to talk her only son out of going up north to college and never coming back. A woman named Dot who did Hattie's hair in those days told her not to feel bad about Ronnie, told her that's what they did when they went away to college. Hattie had followed Dot's advice and trained herself to check the mailbox only once every third day, and then, if she found a card or letter, to save it for a while before she opened it, and then to read it slowly, one page now, another after supper or before she went to bed. (She stopped short of Dot's suggestion that she disconnect her phone so as not to know when they didn't call.)

Recently, however, the situation had changed, at least in regard to her niece Caroline. Hattie had come down the driveway from the cottage to find out who was beeping the horn like a taxi driver in front of the stucco house, and she found a station wagon she'd never seen before—a boxy-looking foreign model with a shiny blue hood and sides dusted red by the trip down the driveway. Hattie could not have been more surprised to discover her niece behind the wheel. Caroline didn't get out of the car at first. She sat and stared out the windshield at the house she grew up in. The windows were broken or covered with rain-spotted dust, the porch nearly buried in a shroud of kudzu, and the stucco had fallen away in patches, so the wooden furring showed through here and there, like bones. In the back seat of the station wagon, a little girl straddled the baggage to get her head out the window. "Mom, you lived *here?*" she was saying. "You *lived* here?"

"Caroline?" Hattie said when she reached the car. She bent over to the driver's side and looked at her niece, whose hair was lighter and curlier than Hattie remembered. "Y'all aren't in Germany like you were."

"No," Caroline said sadly. "We're home."

Hattie was so surprised that she didn't know what else to say. She helped Caroline out of the car, accepted a peck on the cheek, and then they walked back to the cottage behind the big stucco house with Lizbeth trailing after them, kicking up reddish clouds of dust. At the cottage stoop, the child stopped short and said, this time to Hattie, "You live *here?*" From the top of three sagging steps, Hattie looked down at her grandniece—her only grand-anything, for that matter, since Ronnie had never married. In person, Lizbeth looked even more like Caroline at that age than she did in the three school-pictures Hattie had lined up on her refrigerator door. Lizbeth had her mother's pale and serious little face and her pointed chin. She even had the long blond braids, which she kept tossing back over her shoulders. It was a remarkable resemblance—so much so that the sight of Lizbeth in her shorts and halter, squatting to look under the stoop, with her skinny arms wrapped around her knees, made the ground fall away from under Hattie's feet for a moment, made her feel cut loose and drifting in time.

60

"Don't mess around down there," Hattie said. "Might be snakes."

"Really?" said Lizbeth, with interest. Caroline grabbed her hand and hauled her up the steps.

Inside the cottage, while Caroline and Lizbeth looked around at the water-stained ceiling and bulging walls, Hattie cleared her throat. She put her arm around Lizbeth, a little shyly, and said, "You know, your uncle, no, your great-uncle Pete built this little old place way back when he was a carpenter's apprentice." The memory of Pete sprang up in Hattie as she said it, nails fanning out of his mouth, sweating and grumbling at a joint he couldn't keep square or a window that wouldn't level.

"What's a prentice?" Lizbeth asked.

"Somebody who hasn't had much practice yet," said Caroline from the sofa.

Hattie stepped down into her kitchen—a lean-to that used to be a porch—and came back with iced tea and windmill cookies, as ready as she would ever be to answer Caroline's question about why—*oh, why?*—she had moved out of the stucco house. She told them how the pipes had frozen and burst in the house two and a half years ago, while she was gone to visit her brother Ebe in Columbus. "Can you imagine?" Hattie said. "Two degrees above zero? In Georgia?" She told them about the iceberg under the kitchen sink and the frozen waterfall from the bathroom down the front hall stairs. She couldn't open the front door for the ice, she said.

"But broken pipes can be *fixed*, Aunt Hattie," Caroline said. "They can be replaced."

Hattie told them she'd had no choice but to spend the night in the cottage—"with the mice," she said, winking at Lizbeth. She slept on the floor, wrapped up in nearly everything she had in her suitcase, next to the wood stove.

"Oh, Aunt Hattie."

"Lucky thing that old stove was still hooked up to the chimney or I'd like to froze to death," Hattie said. She didn't tell them what she broke up and burned in the stove: first a piece of loose floorboard that she held by one end and stomped on to snap it in two, and then a wooden rocking chair that had belonged to her grandmother. She didn't tell them about waking up in the cottage the next morning, either, with the smell of the river pulling her from sleep, as if it were spring instead of late December. The smell came through the leaky windows, through holes in the roof and cracks in the floor, until she got up stiffly, puzzled. At the window, an almost warm breeze touched her face and bore to her the thick, tangible sweetness of it. Fifty yards beyond the cottage, through dead vines and the black trunks and branches of trees, Hattie saw mist rising from the water. The temperature must have climbed fifty degrees overnight.

And she didn't tell them what she'd thought about, standing at the window, seeing the mist. She thought about Pete, her husband, in his overalls, coming down the drive the way he used to in an orange cloud of dust, stopping where she knelt at the edge of her garden, saying he was off to fetch the fishing poles because the smell of the river was working on him, knocking her straw garden hat over her eyes when he kissed the back of her neck, saying, "Come on, now." And then the weight of the sun on their backs as they walked to the river, and the lifting of it when they reached the trees. If Hattie told Caroline all of that, she would have had to explain how, standing there at the window, she knew that the frozen pipes and the ice that must be melting around the cracked toilet and down the front stairs were a gift to her, something she'd been waiting for all along. Later, when Hattie watched the men carry what she'd sold to the junk dealer out of the stucco house—the mahogany sideboard, cartons full of Ronnie's baseball cards, the spool bed her mother died in—she had felt a breaking up inside her and a sweeping away. For the first time in her life, as she watched the truck lean precariously into the driveway, threatening the safety of a highboy that stuck up over the wooden sides, Hattie Blount knew what it felt like to be the one who was leaving—even if it was only down the driveway to the cottage—instead of the one left behind.

"Well," Caroline said, after the long silence. "I wonder what Leonard is going to think about all of this when he gets home in September."

"Home?" said Hattie. "Here, you mean?" She paused and, with some effort, called to mind Caroline's husband, whom she had met three times in her life. She knew that Leonard played an instrument in the Air Force Band—saxophone, she thought it was—and that he enjoyed asking Hattie to pronounce words like "well" and "whale," or "pin" and "pen," claiming that he couldn't hear the difference the way she said them. It was on his account that Caroline set about learning to speak standard English, she called it, rooting out every "y'all" and "reckon" and "yonder," until she might as well have been from Cleveland or Chicago, where standard English was apparently the native tongue.

"I thought Leonard was from Minnesota," Hattie said.

Caroline explained that Leonard, who was from Michigan, was going to be transferred to Robins Field as of September. "That's in Warner Robins, Aunt Hattie. Didn't you get my letter?"

Hattie thought about the pile of dusty letters on top of the refrigerator. Was there a page somewhere she hadn't read? Then she looked toward the door, where Lizbeth stood scratching her fingernails against the screen. "But where's Leonard now?" Hattie said.

"He's on tour with the band, for heaven's sake. Didn't you hear what I said, Aunt Hattie? Last time I looked, Warner Robins was only *twenty miles from here.*"

Lizbeth spoke up suddenly. She told the screen door she was scratching that she wasn't so sure she wanted to live in Great-aunt Hattie's house anymore, even *with* a new family room and a swimming pool, and by the way, she hadn't seen any swimming pool, and it was *hot*. Taken by surprise once again, Hattie looked at the rash of well-scratched mosquito bites on the child's bare back. "What family room?" she said, and Caroline went out to the car for the magazines.

She brought in two boxes of them—mostly back issues of *Better Homes* and *House Beautiful* whose address labels showed how long she had been making plans: Hickam AFB, Hawaii; Caribou, Maine; Canada, Idaho, APO San Francisco, APO New York. The oldest, most tattered issues had come to her in Newfoundland, where Leonard was first stationed and where the before-and-after kitchens, the tiled baths, and the wallpapering tips had sustained her in the frozen waste. Stuck between the magazines and the side of the box—so that you couldn't miss it—was an ancient-looking sheaf of papers, folded and refolded, and stapled at the corner. Hattie recognized it immediately. Caroline plucked it from the box and laid it in Hattie's lap.

"Remember that?" Caroline said, looking shy all of a sudden.

Hattie unfolded the photocopied deed carefully and smoothed the creases. There, on the appropriate blank, was Caroline's signature, faint but schoolgirl-neat, with Leonard's signature, bolder and more recent, beneath it. Hattie looked at the paper for a while. "Y'all never mailed it back," she said.

"I kept it, though," Caroline said. "Just in case."

"Just in case," said Hattie. A deep, old, empty space seemed to be opening up inside her. Her stomach felt lost in it.

"Offer still hold, Aunt Hattie?"

Hattie looked up at Caroline, who was standing before her, wearing a look on her face that she used to wear when she brought home a carved soap angel for Mother's Day or a clay ashtray wrapped in hand-decorated tissue paper. "Well," said Hattie, slowly and faintly, as if she were saying it to herself, "I guess so."

Caroline looked relieved. She plopped down close to Hattie on the sofa, hugged her hard with one arm, and bent over to pick a particularly dog-eared magazine from the box. She let it fall open across her knees to its most-used page. "Look at this," she said. "Look at what we can *do.*"

Hattie leaned over and looked at the picture Caroline pointed to. It was a very large room, with lots of little bookcases and built-in things that divided it up, all in white, with green plants everywhere. The ceiling of the room was slanted like an attic, but on either side of the peak, sections were lifted up to make two long rows of windows that looked out on a too-blue magazine sky.

"What's this here?" Hattie asked.

"It's the family room!" said Lizbeth, at her elbow now.

Hattie looked at the picture again. "Looks like a attic."

"It *is* an attic," said Caroline. She flipped the page to a smaller photo of a dark, raftered attic like the one in the stucco house. "That's what it used to look like."

Hattie felt her stomach flop in the empty space inside her. She looked at Lizbeth leaning over her left arm and Caroline eager on her right. "Be hotter than blazes up there," she said.

"Insulation, Aunt Hattie. Air conditioning." Caroline sounded happier and happier.

"No windows like that in our attic either."

Caroline was not discouraged. "Oh, that's easy—you just put in dormers, see? It says right here. They cut three sides and jack up a section of the roof like that."

"You cut holes in the roof?" A little frantically, Hattie searched her mind for something and found it. She shook her head. "I doubt you could do that here, Caroline—in the house, I mean. On account of the termites."

Caroline sat back against the cushions. "What termites?"

"*What* termites?" Hattie leaned forward. "You mean you don't recall how we de-fumigated the place? Twice." She frowned. "Maybe the first time was before you were born, when your mama and daddy were still in Raleigh and—"

"Termites," Caroline said. She looked grimly from the magazine picture to a corner of the house that she could see through the window from where she sat. "We'll just see."

The next day she called in a carpenter and had him check the whole house. He was a young man in blue jeans, with a black beard, and Hattie overheard him being sympathetic to Caroline, saying how there was no excuse for letting a fine old home like this go to ruin. He also said that the roof and rafters were as sound as a dollar.

"Well, he's wrong," Hattie said after he left. "I know, because your uncle Pete was a carpenter. He built this old cottage and he fixed that old roof over there more than once, and he *told* me about termites. Once they do their damage, the damage is done."

"Well, *this* carpenter says it's perfectly safe. He says he puts dormers in old houses all the time."

Hattie thought about the carpenter standing in the driveway with Caroline, the two of them shielding their eyes while they looked up at the roof. She had seen him look at the house, then over at the cottage, and then back to Caroline, shaking his head the whole time as if something was a crying shame.

"I wouldn't let that man build me a shoeshine box," Hattie said.

Within a week, they were tearing out walls.

Hattie escaped to the river every morning. She would have taken Lizbeth with her but Caroline said no, so she went alone as usual, setting up her lawn chair, baiting her hook, casting, and waiting. From behind her, slightly muffled by flies and mosquitoes droning, muffled, too, by the curtains of leafy kudzu draped over the trees and spread over the ground until the whole riverbank was green and lumpy as a poorly made bed, came the whine of a drill, the screams of circular saws, the crack-crack crack-crack of multiple hammers.

Most mornings Hattie spent dozing on and off, breathing the river smell. ("What *is* that?" Lizbeth asked one time and Caroline replied, "Rotting vegetation.") But this particular morning, Hattie had barely got herself settled in her chair before a tug on the line brought her to her feet, her heart leaping. The line was reeling out so fast that she couldn't get a hold of the handle—it beat hard against her fingers as it spun. "Whoa," she said. "Hold on!" At last she caught the handle, stopped it, and pulled up sharply on the line to set the hook. She reeled it in a bit, let it run, and reeled it up again, smiling at the little pull of fear that always went with hooking something but you didn't know what. Whatever it was on the line, it was fighting back. She thought hopefully about trout, but it would have to be a mighty big trout. Must be catfish. She squinted at the water to see what she could see. She wound the reel one turn, two, and then it stopped. The line was taut. Try as she might, she couldn't move the handle even half a turn. With a sigh, she jerked the rod up and saw some branches moving farther downriver.

"Well, shoot," she said aloud. "How'd I end up way down there?"

The vegetation was impassable along the bank, so she laid down her rod and waded, shoes and all, into the river, staying close to the bank, following the line hand over hand until she got to the end of it in a clump of willow and reeds. She bent over and pushed branches out of the way to see that she'd got her line wound around what looked like a hairy loaf of bread dough. It was somebody's arm.

*   *   *

"Sometimes they shrivel and sometimes they pop, shrivel and pop, shir-r-riv-el and—" With the last "POP!" Lizbeth leaped off the cottage stoop into the grass.

"Stop it!" her mother snapped. Caroline was pale. The glass of lemonade she held on the arm of the rocking chair trembled.

Hattie was leaning against one of the iron poles that used to hold the roof up, when the stoop had a roof. She looked across the driveway at the pile of debris behind the stucco house. She'd told Caroline to make that carpenter bring a dumpster to the site. Now they had a mountain of broken wallboard, chunks of plaster, and bits of lath from the walls they'd torn out.

"Sit down now, Lizbeth," Hattie said without turning away from the debris, "and hush. Your mother's very upset."

"What's *she* so upset about?"

"It ain't polite to call your mama *she* when she's right there behind you."

"All right. What's my *mother* so upset about? *She* didn't find the guy. You did." Lizbeth picked up her lemonade and sucked it noisily through a straw. "What did the sheriff mean when he said that anyway, sometimes they shrivel and sometimes they pop? What was he talking about, Mom?"

"Hush, Lizbeth," said Hattie.

"I never saw a dead body before," Caroline said.

"I never saw one at *all* because you wouldn't let me," Lizbeth complained.

"It was all puffed up—oh, Aunt Hattie, what if Lizbeth had gone with you this morning?"

"Why would she, Caroline? She never goes fishing with me."

"But what if she had? What if *she* had been the one to find it?"

"Him, you mean."

"What?"

"Drew Johnson was a him."

For a few minutes, no one spoke. Lizbeth took to mouthing almost but not quite silently, "Shrivel and pop. Shrivel and pop." She changed it now and again to "Crackle and pop," and she swung her legs back and forth over the side of the stoop to keep time.

After a while, Hattie said, "Maybe we should've told the sheriff that we locked him out."

"Locked who out?" said Caroline.

"Drew Johnson."

Caroline sat straight up and held her trembling lemonade quite still. "What are you talking about?"

So Hattie told her what, to protect her honor and that of the dead, she had failed to tell the sheriff. Hattie knew exactly how Drew Johnson ended up in the river at the edge of her property because she knew that whenever he got too drunk to go home to his room, where the landlady wouldn't let him in, he spent the night on the floor in Hattie's empty house. When she still lived in the house, he'd spent it in the empty cottage. She had seen him one night from the dining room windows, seen him lurching across the rectangles of yellow light on the driveway, making his way back to the cottage at the rear. She figured out what he was up to—knowing his landlady from church—and, when she moved out of the house, she left the door open for him there instead. After a couple of fumblings against the locked door on the cottage stoop, he understood the exchange.

Lizbeth was thrilled. "You mean the dead guy was in our actual house?"

"You *knew* he was in your house?" Caroline said. "And you never called the police on him?"

Hattie was silent. More than once she'd been tempted to take him some breakfast. "He was an old neighbor, Caroline." She shook her head. "I don't know how I could have let you lock that door."

Now Caroline made a sudden movement that splashed lemonade over the rim of her glass. "Oh, now wait a minute, Aunt Hattie. If you're trying to say it's *my* fault, *I* locked him out—"

"No, no, no, I don't mean that. You didn't know he came here like he did. I knew it, but you didn't."

"Well," said Caroline. "All right then." She sat back a little. Her ice cubes rattled. "But I don't think you should blame yourself either. After all, it's your house, Aunt Hattie. You have a right to lock it up if you want to. He's lucky you didn't do it a long time ago." She took a tentative sip of lemonade. "I would have."

Hattie stared at the stucco house, half-covered now with textured aluminum siding. "I should've told him," she said sadly. "I should've let him know somehow." She hugged her sweater around her. "I'm so sorry," she said. "I forgot about him. I just forgot."

*   *   *

Hattie Blount was not surprised that nobody much came to Drew Johnson's funeral. He was a man who kept to himself, especially in his later years. His wife had left him long ago, and his children, like most children, were scattered. The sheriff probably had the devil of a time trying to notify them. The sheriff was at the funeral, standing with his feet spread apart and his hands folded in front of him. There was a minister, also, and Drew Johnson's landlady, Eleanor Pierce. Hattie gave them a stiff nod as she passed them on her way to the front of the chapel.

When she got up to the casket, she stood before it and waited for the memory to well up inside her, the way it did at every funeral she'd attended in the last thirty years—nineteen of them, counting this one. She didn't have to stop and figure out how long ago Pete's was. She kept track of the years and months, even days, the same way she kept waiting, without knowing she was doing it until something came along to remind her. It was the only triple funeral they'd ever had at Sawyer's Funeral Home—the only one, in fact, that Mr. Sawyer had ever seen—Pete's brother Eddie on the left, Eddie's wife Frances on the right, and Pete in the middle. You could hardly get in the door at that one, but then young people always drew a crowd. Eddie and Frances had been thrown through the windshield, the both of them, so their caskets had to be closed, like Drew's.

But not Pete's. He'd been riding in the back seat—Hattie never found out why, since it was his car and he should have been driving.

The cause of death was a blow to the back of the head. He kept a toolbox on the back shelf by the rear window, and Hattie always pictured how he must have been leaning forward to talk to Eddie and Frances in the front seat and maybe Eddie turned around for a second to look at Pete when the pickup came over the hill in the wrong lane, passing somebody. Hattie figured the toolbox—a little one, but heavy, packed with carpenter's tools and fishing lures—must have hit her husband and then tumbled him head first onto the front seat. There wasn't a scratch on him from the front. He really did look like he was sleeping, just like people always said.

She knew it was not wise to stand here at Drew Johnson's funeral and imagine Pete instead, lying there in the black suit the undertaker provided. (Hattie, with her son in her arms and Caroline holding onto her leg, kept telling people that her husband wouldn't have been caught dead in a suit like that. She must have said it a dozen times. Only one person laughed, nervously.) It wasn't wise to stand here and picture his stern eyebrows and the thin straight line of his mouth that would never be lopsided again, and the black suit coat, as still as if it were wood or granite under there instead of a man's chest. Hattie thought that was the worst thing about him lying there, the way he looked like himself, only more official somehow, but if you put your hand near the suit coat your fingers felt a chill, and if you dared to touch the breast pocket, all you felt was something cold, hard, and hollow.

A couple of feet away from Drew Johnson's casket, Hattie felt her knees wobble and her palms grow damp. She looked over her shoulder. The sheriff, standing at ease behind the last row of empty folding chairs, nodded to her and turned back to his conversation with the undertaker. Eleanor Pierce, the brim of her felt hat quivering, was engrossed by the minister.

Nobody was looking. Hattie reached out and ran her hand along the glossy wooden lid of the casket. Her sweaty fingertips left four streaks that faded slowly, almost without a trace.

*   *   *

In the middle of the night after Drew Johnson's funeral, Hattie Blount untangled the sweaty sheets wound around her legs and got up from the sofa. She put on her robe and walked out across the grass and up the driveway to the stucco house. The big front doors were locked so she went around to the back, stopping by the heap of trash to pick out a two-foot length of two-by-four, which she carried under her arm like a rifle. She wondered if Drew Johnson had tried the back.

Inside, she paid no mind to the blue-and-white kitchen or the new chandelier but moved by moonlight up the carpeted stairs. She felt funny and floating as she ascended, probably because there used to be a wall where there was now a polished banister. Caroline liked the grace and drama of an open stairway, she said.

In the attic, Hattie stood very still, the heat pressing up against her, and waited until her eyes grew accustomed to the milky light from the window. Looking up, she saw on a rafter the beginning of a chalk line the carpenters had drawn to show them where to wield the saw. The end of the line got lost in the blackness under the peak of the roof. Hattie hefted her two-by-four like a base-ball bat, stepped up to a beam installed between floor and rafters, and gave it a good, hard *whack*. The two-by-four flew out of her hands, but the beam held. The roof stayed up. Not so much as a tremor in it. Hattie rubbed her smarting palms on her thighs. "So much for termites," she said. For a moment, she thought she might cry.

Then a gleam on the floor near the far attic window caught her eye. She moved cautiously toward it in the darkness until, almost there, her bare toe stubbed something cool and smooth that fell over and rolled away. It was a bottle—three bottles in all—and, on the floor beside them, a matchbox that rattled when she picked it up and dropped it into her pocket. She carried the bottles, one in each hand and one under her arm, to the window, where she read the labels: *Jack Daniels* (empty), *Jack Daniels* (half-empty), and *Jim Beam* (unopened). When she held the empty bottle up to the moon-light, something inside it shifted against the glass with a sound like dried grass. *Termite!* she thought, although it could as well have been a beetle or a roach. She shook the bottle and the insect crumbled to pieces. Sometimes they shrivel, she thought. She gathered the bottles and hurried down the stairs.

In the kitchen she opened the Jim Beam and splashed it on the floor, on the wallpaper, on the built-in desk. She made a little river of whiskey—opening the second bottle—out the back door, down the steps, all the way to the trash heap, which was too close to the house for burning, as she had pointed out one time to Caroline. She placed the termite bottle on the pile of debris and walked solemnly around it, stopping every few steps to sprinkle a little Jack Daniels on the heap. Then she lit a match.

*   *   *

Caroline caught her, though. Caught her out there in her bathrobe at three in the morning—a tall woman with wild gray hair and a face crinkled and glistening in the heat, reeking of whiskey, burning the trash. Caroline hauled out the hose and put out the fire and told her aunt that if she didn't leave off about termites and go straight in to bed Caroline would have to call the sheriff and have him escort her to jail or the loony bin, whichever came first.

It didn't come to that. Hattie went peaceably to bed, and, in the morning, took her lawn chair and fishing rod to the riverbank as usual.

She was still there, waiting, when the neighbors Caroline invited from the subdivision came to watch the carpenter and his assistants jack up the roof, one side at a time, like wings, said the carpenter, like the house was damned near ready to take off and fly away to someplace in particular. She was still waiting when she heard the hiss of the hydraulic jack, the terrible creaking and groaning, and then the crash, which went on and on, the powdery roar of it pierced by shouts and cries, as carpenters jumped for their lives, and the termite-weakened ridgepole fell through the termite-weakened floor, and the floor collapsed into a bedroom that was missing a support wall, until two whole stories landed on the open stairway and the wallpapered kitchen. When silence fell, broken only by coughing and the shifting of debris, the house looked like a shoe box stepped on by a giant foot. Hattie didn't run right up the bank to see, but she knew, in a flash, why she had forgotten to bait her hook this morning.

Self Storage

The Bag Lady & the Country Band

The country western band was the beginning of the end for me and Nutty Squirrel. I should have known it the first time their van pulled into the parking lot with all its windows broken and the ghost of the words "Forever Green Landscapes" bleeding through brown paint on the sides. We've had runaway teenagers out here, migrant workers, illegal immigrants, bag ladies and gentlemen, a battered wife, a farmless farm family from out near Mechanicsville, and a gang of sneak thieves who used 44E to stash their loot. We had a punk rock group back in 1984—their van said "Presto Pest Control," which turned out to be the name of the group—but we never had a country western band before. Lola said I should have seen it coming.

Knucklehead they call themselves. It fits. Four big guys, and it took them more than an hour to move their stuff into 9W, a twelve-by-twelve-foot unit they jam-packed with at least ten speaker cabinets—all big enough to blow your eardrums out—not to mention keyboards, mike stands, amplifiers, drums, a soundboard studded with knobs and switches, and lights. Thousands and thousands of watts' worth. If they ever figured out a way to plug in all those lights at once, we'd have a blackout up and down the frontage road this side of the interstate, from Randy's RVs to the standardized testing company. They also have a smoke machine. I couldn't tell it was a smoke machine from across the parking lot when they were moving in, but Lola spotted it right away. "Look at that," she said to me. "They have a smoke machine." I worried about the alarms going off, but Lola said it wasn't that kind of smoke. What's a country band doing with a smoke machine, anyway? I asked her. Why all the electronics? Whatever happened to Hank Williams, Sr., and Patsy Cline?

"They're dead," said Lola.

"What about Willie Nelson, for God's sake?" You couldn't picture Willie Nelson with a smoke machine. I couldn't, anyway.

Lola said, "Times change."

Lola stores a whole household's worth of furniture in 27E. She was in graduate school studying the Philosophical Origins of Contemporary Thought when she discovered the first lump in her breast three years ago. She was thirty-three then. She specialized in guys like Kneecha and Highdigger, whose names she misspells more or less phonetically. A small act of rebellion, she calls it. In the flurry of medical procedures that followed her discovery, her dissertation languished, and philosophy began to seem like a cruel joke anyway, so she stopped paying tuition and got herself a job at the standardized testing company up the road. She started out as a test editor, using her obscure knowledge to find sample reading passages guaranteed to confound the average high school junior, but in the next year and a half she had too many rounds of radiation and chemotherapy to hold down more than a temporary job. They moved her to the Test Registration Department in the basement. She opens envelopes there. She takes the registration forms full of endless dots out of the envelopes to see if each dot has been darkened completely with a Number Two pencil. Lola's not the only former Ph.D. candidate opening envelopes down there.

But here's the interesting part. Do you know what happens if you screw up when you fill out your standardized test registration form? if you make stray marks? if you don't erase completely or use a Number Two pencil to make your marks heavy and black? You know what happens? *They fix it for you.* That's right. After all those warnings in boldface all-capital letters, if the computer can't read your dots they give your registration form to Lola—or to any one of the dozens of actual human beings sitting at long tables in a big, windowless room with piles of official brown envelopes to the left of them and computer terminals glowing to their right—and one of them, after ensuring that your check is made out for the proper amount, personally enters your data into the great Central Processing Apparatus. Do as you're told and you get computer-processed. Screw up and they turn you over to the human beings. It's something to think about.

75

The country band makes a terrific amount of noise. I suppose they figure they've got no neighbors out here to call the police on them. (The standardized testing company doesn't count; Lola says it's so hermetically sealed and secure in there that a cruise missile could land in the parking lot and nobody in Test Registration would know it until quitting time.) So the Knuckleheads feel free to practice as loud as they please on Tuesdays and alternate Thursdays, and with their loading up the truck on Friday after-noons and bringing everything back on Sunday, it seems as though they're always around, we never have a moment's peace. The Tuesday/Thursday noise drove out the Bag Lady in 26w—who pretended to the end that we didn't know she was there and vice versa. Lola, who likes the country band, said, well, if the Bag Lady preferred the Muzak in the bus station to live country tunes, then let her go. I pointed out that an aversion to hearing "Take Me Back to Tulsa" taken from the top over and over again said nothing about the Bag Lady's taste, or lack of it, in music. Lola countered by reminding me that it was dehumanizing to call the Bag Lady a bag lady anyway.

"Her name is Emily," Lola said.

"How do you know?" I asked her.

"I saw it on her luggage tag," she said.

"How do you know she didn't pick that suitcase out of a dumpster?"

"It's on her Bible, too."

Now who's violating Bag Lady Emily's human dignity here, I wanted to know: me, because I have to call her something, or Lola, who feels free to dig around in her things?

"I wasn't digging around," Lola said. "The Bible and the suit-case were both right out in the open."

"Out in the open behind closed doors," I said, which wasn't really fair of me since I, too, go around to all the officially unoccupied storage units now and again to make sure nobody's dead in any of them or doing anything seriously illegal.

76

Lola, whose perfect eyebrows had grown back in, raised the left one with disdain and said, "If you'd quit complaining long enough, I could show you how to two-step to that music. 'Light feet,'" she added, quoting Kneecha, "'are the first attribute of divinity.'"

With that, she left for work, leaving me to ponder a sobering question: If I couldn't find peace (never mind quiet or solitude) out here at Nutty Squirrel's Self-Storage Mini-Warehouse, among the orphaned things, the homeless goods, the forgotten objects of America, where the heck was I going to find it?

The Company of Things

This is the kind of thing that can happen. For fifteen years I dissected cockroaches in Dr. Derkson's lab to study certain characteristics of their tiny brains. (Human brains have over six hundred million synapses per cubic millimeter of cortex, whereas cockroaches have less than a cubic millimeter of brain all together, but ask yourself this: which is better at holding its territory?) I was Professional Scientific Staff, Researcher III, which means I made a nice little salary, enough to pay the mortgage, the taxes, the insurance, the car payments, the utilities, the telephone bill, the charge cards, and several magazine subscriptions. Then, in 1982, our NIH grant didn't get renewed. Too many labs studying cockroach brains, we heard, though Derkson was crazy enough to insist that animal rights people had something to do with it. Anyway, the lab was kaput. Principal Investigator Derkson was tenured faculty, but I was out the door. Luckily, I didn't have a family counting on me. I tightened my belt and updated my resumé. For two and a half years, the old man wrote me glowing recommendations—couldn't say enough about how skilled and reliable I was—but labs were downsizing all over the place, and when an opening did crop up, there were always ten other people as qualified as I was, and five of them were just as personable, and three were female, and two were better looking, and one of them got the job. My unemployment ran out in six months, then my savings, and then my Principal Investigator killed himself, so there went my recommendations. I resorted to selling things, starting with the motorcycle and ending with the house. I never expected to fall into my life's work when I went to rent a place to store my meager furnishings, but one look at my stuff nestled in the little concrete cubicle that was mine for a mere ten dollars a month in those days, and I knew I was saved. I didn't have to share a bedroom in a house full of dental students. There was a place for me in storage.

Nutty Squirrel in Coralville, where I'm manager-slash-nightwatchperson, is my third location and the best setup so far. At other places, I've had to move from unit to vacant unit, taking my padlock with me and improvising my internal security—all too often, nothing but a steel drum or piece of heavy furniture on the inside in front of the door. At Nutty Squirrel, the manager-slash-nightwatchperson gets a free storage cubicle of his or her very own. Of course I'm not supposed to *live* in it, but as long as I do my job—keep everything secure, answer the beeper fast enough to prevent people from kicking in the door when they've lost their keys or forgotten their combinations (which I try to keep on file in the office), and occasionally harass a renter for nonpayment—the owner doesn't care where I live. He's seen the barn board I put up over the concrete blocks in One West, and he's never said a word. So I get a private but not, alas, soundproof place to lay my head, free of charge, and there's none of this driving to work everyday either—another good thing, since I no longer have a cycle or a car. I shower at the truck stop, use the washroom in the front office, and take my meals where I please. In the winter, I come home from the heated office out front and burrow into a fat, down-filled sleeping bag for the night. I get a lot of reading done in the winter.

The one thing I would change out here, though, if I could change anything, is the sign, which is up on top of a long pole, so you can see it from the interstate. The logo is supposed to be the silhouette of a squirrel, but it looks as much like a curled-up human fetus as a hoarding squirrel. It's like the picture my mother used to have on top of her TV of a cow that turns into the face of Jesus if you reverse your perception of figure and ground. I don't know how many times I drove by this place (when I still had wheels) and wondered what kind of business would have a fetus for a logo, when one day my brain shifted into a different gear and I got the picture. The only trouble is, once you see the fetus, it's hard to turn it back into a squirrel.

My friend Lola used to ask me if I didn't feel lonely out here sometimes, if I didn't feel like an intruder among other people's goods. Nothing, I told her, could be farther from the truth. I have always enjoyed the company of things. I feel more at home in self storage than I've felt since I was small enough to crawl through the little door at the back of my parents' bedroom closet into the only scrap of attic we had in our Cape Cod. It was a close, dry, dusty crawl space full of *things:* pictureless picture frames, battered luggage, suits in plastic garment bags, records no one listened to, yearbooks from my mother's high school, plaid and pleated uniforms my older sister had outgrown, and toys not quite broken enough to throw away—a three-wheeled dump truck, an ancient doll whose porcelain face was cracked from inner eyebrow to upper lip. There were books that smelled like books, beams that smelled like dry-rotting beams, and a long-forgotten Sunbeam toaster in the carton it came in. There were cardboard boxes bent into trapezoids and parallelograms, their box bottoms littered with reassuring stuff— a chess piece, a pencil stub, a Jack of Spades, a screw, a lump of modeling clay, a spool of red thread, most of it unwound and tangled around the other things in the box, everything coated with dust and disuse. Under the peak of the roof, a window shaped like a stop sign let in gray light, except for a circular spot I had cleaned with spit. The round, clean spot on the glass let in a beam full of dust motes that fell like a spotlight on this thing or that, depending on the time of day. It could make a bright white circle on a gray suit or a cherry red spot on a suitcase of maroon leather. No matter how long I stared, I could never decide which color the suitcase really was, or whether the somber gold drapes folded carefully over those hangers were really bright yellow like the spot of light, and not somber gold at all. Lola said that it was very postmodern of me to believe only in the surfaces of things.

I used to spend whole afternoons in the storage place under the eaves when I was a kid. Eventually, my mother would open the door and call through the closet, "Sweetheart, what are you doing in there—gathering dust?" And you know something? That's exactly what I was doing. I was sitting on the floor among those things, hardly breathing, finding it harder and harder, as the light got grayer, to tell where they left off and I began, waiting for the blanket of dust that coated everything else to gather on arms and legs that might be mine or might not.

When I described all this to Lola, she said it sounded to her as if I'd come darn close to experiencing what Highdigger called the Radical Astonishment of Being. "Especially that part about the stuff in the bottoms of the boxes," she said. "You were in touch with Is-ness and What-ness for sure. On the other hand," she added, shrugging her narrow shoulders, "maybe you were autistic."

This led us into a little argument. I said that people who are autistic don't outgrow it, just like that. I know a thing or two about biology and brain development after all.

"Who said anything about outgrowing it?" said Lola. "Look around you, bud." She was sitting in her Queen Anne wing chair, surrounded by all the other furniture and knickknacks and whatnots she had inherited from her aunt and stored in cubicle 27E for lack of a house big enough to put it in. I was sitting on a hope chest at her feet. I reminded her that I didn't always live in storage.

"No. Before this, you spent fifteen years in a one-man lab with cockroaches."

When I pointed out that she *almost* had a degree in philosophy, not psychology, she laughed and patted my knee and told me that she didn't need a degree in psychology to recognize living in a self-storage cubicle as a transparent attempt on my part to return to the womb. And then, when I maintained that my little concrete room was, if anything, more like a *tomb* than a *womb*, she tossed her bald head so that her sailor cap slid down and bumped into her ear. "Womb, tomb," she said. "What's the difference?"

I figured I had no choice then but to tell her about the crucial printing error in my first *Missal for Little Catholics*. It was in the Hail Mary, in the part that goes "Blessed is the fruit of thy womb, Jesus." For some reason—human error? mechanical failure? divine intervention?—the "w" was missing. Blessed is the fruit of thy o-m-b, it said. This would have caused me no confusion, since I already knew the Hail Mary by heart, if I hadn't learned the line wrong in the first place. Like everybody else in the first grade, I thought it went: "Blessed is the Fruit of the Loom, Jesus." When I saw "o-m-b" in my *Missal for Little Catholics,* the first thing I did was to secretly consult my underpants and confirm my suspicions that "Loom" did not, in fact, end with a "b."

I wracked my brain for a rhyming word that did. *Blank-o-m-b,* I needed. "Comb" was out, I knew that much, and "womb" would not have occurred to me in a million years, but it didn't take me too long to come up with "tomb," since the thing that had always impressed me most about Jesus was not the whole story about how He suffered and died for our sins or even that He rose from the dead and ascended into heaven, but that He'd spent three whole days alone in that tomb. I could identify with that. So "tomb" it was. It made a certain kind of sense: Blessed is the fruit (well, the fruit was still a puzzle) of thy tomb, Jesus. I told Lola how I used to sit in my own storage space behind my parents' bed and think about *Him*—sitting on a stone slab in the cool, cool dark, all wrapped in white linen and festooned with apples and grapes.

By the time I finished telling this story, Lola looked very serious, her eyes as huge as they always were after a round of chemo, when her fine-boned face got thinner than ever and all her hair fell out. After a long silence, she said it was no accident, this womb/tomb mixup of mine. She said maybe I was smarter than I looked.

The Apex of Western Civilization

You have to think of Lola as a convert to self storage. When I first met her, she hated the whole concept. I was doing my rounds late one afternoon when I pulled up the overhead door to 27E, wondering what happened to the padlock, and there she was, sitting in her aunt's wing chair in the midst of all the stuff she'd inherited, sitting there bald as a billiard ball and so pale that she almost seemed to be glowing in the light from the door. She took me by surprise—there was no car in the parking lot and of course I didn't know that she worked at the standardized testing company, a five-minute walk from Nutty Squirrel. Before I could say "Excuse me," she launched right in as if she'd been expecting me.

"So," she said, "is this the culmination of western civilization?"

I looked around. She continued.

"Have we reached here, in this place, the apex of enlightenment? Is this the peak of human dignity and individual freedom toward which our history has tended—no, *striven*—for five thousand years?" She paused dramatically, giving me a chance to wonder what she was talking about, and then, as if she'd read my mind, she said, "I'm talking about *this*, this edifice full of treasure, this—this—*shrine* to the accumulation of goods." (She waved her hand at a framed Nativity scene done in seashells on top of her aunt's dresser.) "I ask you. Is this place really so different from the pyramids of Egypt or the temples of the Aztecs? From the well-furnished tombs of ancient kings?"

She paused again and looked at me so expectantly that I said, "I don't know. Is it?"

"You're damn right it is!" she said, smacking the velvet arm of the wing chair with her fist. I stepped back a little in the open doorway, thinking that she looked fiery, like Katherine Hepburn—a younger, balder Katherine Hepburn. She leaned toward me, narrowing her eyes, and asked with Hepburn scorn, "And do you know why? Do you know what makes this concrete box so different from the pyramids?"

This, I hoped, was a rhetorical question, but the silence that followed was so long that I knew she expected another answer. I ventured one.

"No mummy inside?"

She went stiff with indignation at that, then collapsed back into her chair like a dropped marionette. She was silent for so long afterward that I started to back out, reaching for the door to pull it down behind me. Usually I try to leave people alone out here, figuring that if they've resorted to spending the afternoon at Nutty Squirrel, the chances are good that they're not looking for human company. I had pulled the door almost to the ground when her voice rose again from the gloom behind it.

She asked, "Did you say *mummy* or *dummy?*"

I knew right then we'd get along.

Citizens of El Salvador

Until the country band came along the only problem I ever had with illegals was making the Salvadorans understand about their cooking fire. That was in 1985, maybe '86. Let me tell you, the first time I noticed smoke curling out of a surprising little hole in the back of the east shed, right under the roof, I panicked. I was *that* close to calling the fire department, but I grabbed an extinguisher instead and kicked open their unlocked door—a side opener not an overhead—nozzle at the ready.

There were thirteen people in 19E at the time—three men, four women, and six children, with one green card among them that they bought from the guy who brought them north—and they all dove, screaming, for the corners of the room. Mothers shielded children, crying *"No matarnos! Por favor—no matarnos!"* Babies wailed. Children wept. Smoke from the scattered twigs and charcoal filled the cubicle, making it hard to see and harder to breathe. Overhead, near the door that stood open behind me, a smoke alarm beeped frantically.

"What does it mean," Lola asked me much later, when I told her the story, *"no matarnos?"*

"It means, 'Don't kill us.'"

"Jesus," she said. "What did you do *then?*"

I ushered the whole group, all of us coughing and sniffling from the smoke, out into the alley. They huddled in a clump, children against the wall, adults shielding them, while I held up the fire extinguisher so they could see what it was. The panic subsided almost instantly, to the point where a young man and two small children followed me back inside and stood near the doorway while I sprayed the remnants of the fire, ruining their dinner. When I turned around, they were all crowded in and around the doorway, looking accusatory now. One of the women was saying something, but the smoke alarm was screaming so loudly over our heads that I couldn't hear what. I saw a man signal to a teenaged boy, who emerged from the crowd in the doorway and dragged a Louis Quatorze chair from a corner to a spot directly beneath the smoke alarm. The chair belonged in the cubicle next door with a lot of other antiques owned by a radiologist who was on sabbatical in Europe and had removed all of his more valuable furniture to storage before leasing his house to interns. The movers had forgotten the chair on their truck until after they'd already locked the other stuff up, so they put the chair in the neighboring cubicle—the one now occupied by the Salvadorans—and took off. I saw the whole thing from the office, but the radiologist had declined to reveal his padlock combination for the office files, so there was nothing I could do for his chair. Anyway, in less than a second the boy had jumped up on the chair, tugged the battery out of the alarm, and handed it to me, leaving two dusty footprints on the brocade seat. Now I could hear the woman, who had taken to repeating for my ignorant Anglo ears, *"La cena! La cena!"* as she pointed to the tortillas mixed up with the remains of the cooking fire.

"La cena?" Lola said.

"The dinner."

"What did you do then?" Lola asked.

"I went out to Kentucky Fried and bought them a couple of buckets."

"Is that all?" she said.

"And something to drink."

"I mean, didn't you feel as though you had to do something about them?"

Of course I had to do something. I introduced myself to the man who seemed to be the father of the boy who left the footprints on the chair. He shook my hand and thanked me for my kindness on behalf of the others. "We are citizens of El Salvador," he confided. Then I went down to 32E and got them a microwave. The guy had a dozen of them in there, just sitting. All different brands. Probably stolen goods. I took one that was still in the box, just in case there was something wrong with the other ones. I didn't want to irradiate the citizens of El Salvador. They'd had enough to put up with already.

Bomb Shelter

The way the Salvadorans hugged the wall, shielding their children while the smoke alarm squealed, reminded me of the air raid drills we used to have at school when I was a kid, I told Lola. We had a bomb shelter in our basement, too. This was in the late fifties, when cars had fins like rockets and practically every basement had a bomb shelter, even if it was only the fruit cellar stocked with cans of beans and tuna and bottles of water, and maybe a chemical toilet tucked under a shelf in a corner. Crematoriums they were—or would have been in the event of a bomb—but everybody pretended they were shelters. The same way we pretended there was a point to having air raid drills at school, with the little kids lined up facing the walls on either side of the long corridor, away from the windows—so as not to be cut by flying glass—and the big kids standing over the little ones, their arms folded over their heads, everybody facing the wall, our eyes closed tight, so as not to be blinded by the Big Flash. I remember the cool tiles of the wall on my cheek, the sour breath of a sheltering seventh grader who'd had chocolate milk for lunch, the heat of another body so close to mine. To distract myself from overwhelming terror, I used to construct elaborate daydreams in which I got everyone—my mother, my sister, my father and his newspaper, and, after a frantic search through the neighborhood while sirens wailed, Blackie, our dog, a beagle-cocker spaniel mix—into the fruit cellar just in time.

Womb or tomb. Take your pick.

Lola the Lopsided

When Lola is not feeling so great, she says things like, "You've heard of Pliny the Elder and Richard the Lionhearted? Well, just call me Lola the Lopsided."

Richard I've heard of. The other guy, no. "Lola," I say, "everybody's lopsided. One way or another."

She says, "Shit. What are we here for, anyway?"

I'm ready for that one. "We're gathering dust," I say. "Just like everything else."

Lola sits looking at her legs, which are stretched out in front of her on the warm asphalt next to mine. Our backs are pressed against the wall of the west shed, whose concrete blocks hold the heat of the sun for hours, even after dark. The sun is almost down now—nothing left but a red blaze along the tree line like a half-filled glass of tomato juice.

After a long time of sitting, watching the tomato juice pale and our legs grow gray and fuzzy at the edges, Lola says, "Dusk."

"I beg your pardon?"

"We are gathering dusk," she says.

Mirage

Every year, in July and August, when there's seed corn to detassel and apples to pick, Nutty Squirrel fills up with migrant workers. The majority are from Mexico, as far as I can tell, some of them strictly seasonal, others in more or less permanent flight from a life of assembling computer keyboards and garage door openers in factories along the wrong side of the border. "We're like a stop on their Underground Railroad," Lola used to like to say, knowing very well how nervous that kind of talk makes me.

Until the country band showed up, I never had a lick of trouble with my guests from south of the border—except for the one cooking fire incident. I was never even sure when one group left and another arrived, they were so discreet. Three months after Knucklehead moved in, things started to change. People started to get careless. I remember waking early one morning in July—a little after four o'clock, as a matter of fact—to the faraway strumming of a guitar. It was pitch black inside, except for the red numbers on my clock, and for a moment, I didn't know where I was. When you don't have anything else to go on, a sound like a strumming guitar can conjure up a whole world for you. In that first moment of waking, if the door had flung open on the corkscrew streets of Toledo or a boulevard in Barcelona, or maybe a tree-lined plaza with a great big fountain in the middle and a volcano or two rising in the background, I wouldn't have been a bit surprised. As it was, I hardly had time to remember that I was stretched out on my futon in One West, and to conclude that the Knuckleheads must have somebody new and uncharacteristically talented in their lineup, before the guitar was joined by a new sound. This was a hollow, melodic clopping like a xylophone or a marimba. It was wonderful. It couldn't be the Knuckleheads, I thought, as I looked at the clock. Then I remembered that the Mexican detasselers set out by five every morning for the Kmart parking lot, where an old school bus picks up workers and takes them to the cornfields for the day. They must have figured that nobody would hear them at this hour. It was careless of them. Uncharacteristic. I listened for a while, picturing the fountain and the volcanoes. Then I rolled over and went back to sleep.

Heresy Alfredo

This is typical. Lola comes around the corner and down my alley all excited, with *Webster's Ninth New Collegiate* open in her arms, struggling to keep the wind from turning the fluttering pages on her, looking, in fact, as if that fat blue book is the only thing keeping her from blowing away herself.

"Look at this!" she says.

"It's a dictionary!" I say.

"But *listen*."

I pat the spot beside me and she slides down to sit against the wall. When Lola worked in the Test Editing Department at the standardized testing company, where they actually make up some of the questions, she was always on the lookout for challenging reading passages and tricky vocabulary words. Now that she's moved down to Test Registration, all she needs for her work are a computer keyboard and a letter opener, but she keeps the dictionary at her side out of habit and peruses it at half-hour intervals, when she and the rest of the envelope-opening, data-entering crew take a two-minute eye-saving break from their monitor screens. Sometimes, if she finds something interesting, she sends it upstairs to her friends and former colleagues in Test Editing. Usually, she just shows it to me.

"I'm listening," I say.

"'Manichean,'" she reads.

I say, "What?"

Lola is patient with me. "Man-uh-KEY-un," she says again, spells it, and goes on: "'A believer in a syncretistic religious dualism originating in Persia in the third century A.D. and teaching'"—she pauses to get my utmost attention—"'*the release of the spirit from matter* through asceticism.'"

"Ah," I say, unsure if she said "asceticism" or "aestheticism." Also unsure which one is which. I figure this could be about fasting or about art.

She gives me a fleeting frown. "Now," she says, raising one eyebrow. "Listen to *this*." And she reads: "'mani*cotti:* tubular pasta shells that may be stuffed with ricotta cheese or *meat;* also,'" she finishes rapidly, "'a dish of stuffed manicotti usually with tomato sauce.'" Letting the dictionary rest in her lap, she looks up at me with shining eyes. "*Manichean, manicotti,*" she repeats, enunciating like the teacher she should have been. "*What* do they have in common?"

"They're right next to each other in the dictionary."

"True," she says, tapping the page in front of her with one long red fingernail. I can see both words there in her lap—first the heresy, then the pasta. "But there's more to it than that," she says. "In the one, the ineffable spirit is trapped within matter, right?"— she pauses long enough for me to think, *That would be the Manichean*—"and in the other, a neat reversal, meat is enclosed within slippery white walls of pasta." *The manicotti.* She beams. I'm lost, but I nod sagely. "Furthermore," she says, practically beside herself with cleverness and delight, "if manicotti is to meat what matter is to spirit, then a parallel exists as well between *antimatter* and *antipasto!*"

"Are they going to put that on a test?" I ask her. I'm picturing those questions with a colon in the middle and a word on either side.

"They might," she says, closing the *Ninth New Collegiate* with a triumphant *thunk.*

I'm glad I'm not a junior in high school.

STEFANIAK

Patsy Cline

On another night, not long after I turned out the light to lie in the dark and worry about Lola, who'd spent the day at Mercy Hospital for tests to decide if she could get by with a lumpectomy this time and a round of radiation, all of a sudden I heard Patsy Cline singing "I Fall to Pieces." The voice was strong and hard and clear as glass, but there was something odd about it. I'd heard the Knuckleheads play this tape at least a dozen times, and yet—*something* was different here. It hit me. Patsy Cline has backup vocals and a band, but this voice was singing by itself, to itself, doing a perfect imitation of all the sadness in the world. It wasn't Patsy Cline. Whoever it was had just stopped singing in midverse. Now *that* reminded me of the country band. Could I be hearing an audition? I sat up, thinking that I owed it to the woman who owned that voice to go out there and tell her that she was much too good to be a Knucklehead.

She started singing something else—in Spanish—and a guitar and marimba came in. I got up and opened my overhead door, lifting it three or four inches, the better to hear. The voice didn't seem to be coming from the country band's cubicle. It was from somewhere down at the other end of the alley where it intersects with the south storage shed. It occurred to me that this was Friday night and the Knuckleheads had packed up and left for the Dance-Mor hours ago. I listened to two more songs—"Stand By Your Man" and another tune the band liked to practice—and then I heard some fool tearing up the frontage road at twice the speed anybody should be going on that gravel. The Forever Green van pulled into my view, shot through the parking lot, and barreled down the alley toward the Knuckleheads' unit. It stopped, engine running. A door squealed open and slammed shut on a steady stream of cussing from somebody who sounded as if he'd had a few too many already. Somebody else was trying to shush him. Apparently they'd been sent to pick up something they forgot.

"Why the hell should I be quiet?" the first guy complained. "Think I'm gonna wake up some of the goddam junk they got stored out here? All these goddam people ain't got the brains to get

88

rid of junk they don't need, no sir, they pay good money to keep it out here, so why the—"

"Shut up, for Christ's sake, and listen," said the other guy.

The voice had gone back to singing "I Fall to Pieces." Absolute silence from the two Knuckleheads now, then some whispers. Being only human, I pushed my door up an inch or two more. Before long, two pairs of cowboy boots clomped past. When I heard them far enough away, I pushed the door up and looked out in time to see the drummer—a lanky guy in jeans and boots and a striped western shirt with the creases still in it—walking slowly, like a man in a dream, around the corner at the end of the alley, in search of Patsy Cline.

Visiting Hours

Before Lola got out of the hospital, Teresa Maldonado had joined the country band, along with the Ramirez twins: Jorge on guitar and Hector—well, Hector played a wooden box full of gourds arranged to produce an octave and a half of tones that sounded like a marimba. Both twins sang back up. They didn't have to know the song. They could pick up a phrase or two and harmonize it, just like that.

Lola's doctors had tried the lumpectomy—a word that will appear as the wrong answer on multiple-choice vocabulary tests across the nation for decades to come—but things had gotten complicated somehow, so she was stuck in the hospital for more than a week. To cheer her up, I brought her a practice tape of Teresa, who could hardly speak a word of English, wailing "Stand by Your Man" with no trace of an accent, while the Ramirez twins took turns trading licks with the steel player. I told her we had eight cubicles full of migrants at last count and they all opened their doors and spilled out into the alleys during Knucklehead rehearsals. "We had a regular street dance going last Thursday," I told Lola. "Not just the Mexicans but kids getting off work from Hy-Vee and Kmart—there must have been thirty people." I was pretty nervous about it. "I mean, where do those Hy-Vee kids think the Mexicans came from?"

Lola lay back on her pillows. She had a transparent look about her that I hadn't seen before and a book—not the dictionary—lying open in her lap. "Those kids don't care if the Mexicans dropped out of the sky," she said. "Now listen to this." And she read: "'The human nervous system develops from a hollow tube of tissue.'" She looked up at me and repeated, "A hollow tube." I recognized her book as one that Dr. Derkson had given me when I worked in the lab: a hardcover edition of *Neuronal Man* that Lola must have borrowed. She hoisted it and said, "There's more: 'A groove appears on the surface of the blastula. The groove deepens, the sides of the groove curling up until they meet at the top, and the neural tube is formed.'" She let the book go and looked at me. "Did you know that—about the neural tube?"

"Well, sure," I said. It was pretty basic information. "From the neural tube, of course, you get your spinal cord and brain developing, and then—"

Lola interrupted. "Then Roussel was right," she said.

"Rue Sell?"

"Not just Roussel. All of them. They were right."

"Right about what?"

"Way deep down inside," Lola said slowly, "human beings are entirely superficial. We are—a surface, curled up into a tube. A *hollow* tube." She looked at me.

"Like manicotti," I said, thinking that would lighten her up.

She looked stunned. "Like manicotti," she said.

"Well," I said briskly, "maybe what you say is true, in a manner of speaking," but Lola wasn't listening to me.

"It's the Absolute Emptiness of Being," she said. Her skin was luminous, as if backlit from the inside. "Right here in a biology book. Who would have thought?"

The Bridge

When I told Lola about Teresa and the Ramirez twins joining the band, I made it sound pretty friendly, but the fact was that plenty of arguments preceded the decision. The steel player wasn't sure he wanted to split the money even *one* more way (except for Bo the drummer, the Knuckleheads saw no problem in regarding Teresa, Jorge, and Hector as a single unit when it came to payroll). The drummer offered repeatedly to put one of his sticks right through the steel player's head, in one ear and out the other. "Shouldn't hurt him a bit," the drummer said.

Once they got the finances figured out, there was still the problem of Teresa's teeth. She couldn't have been more than twenty-four or twenty-five years old, but she had four teeth missing on the top—not counting molars—and three missing on the bottom, and the ones that remained were multicolored. No fluoride in the water in Mexico. No toothbrushes, either, I guess—at least not where Teresa comes from. With her mouth shut she was a sweet-faced woman with rich brown skin and black wavy hair that touched her shoulders. When she opened her mouth, all you saw were the gaps.

"So now we gotta buy her dentures?" the steel player complained.

"Just a bridge," said Bo the drummer.

She needed two, one for the top and one for the bottom. I had a bad feeling, watching from the office as Teresa and the drummer drove off in his station wagon the following Saturday, with one of the Ramirez twins in the back seat as chaperone—or maybe as bodyguard. For more than a decade my, shall we say, neighbors and I had been pretending, in strict observance of self-storage protocol, that we didn't really exist. Teresa and the twins, along with all the people who opened their doors and even ventured out into the alleys during country band rehearsals, had abandoned the pretense. On rehearsal nights, I could only hope that cars on the interstate sped by too quickly for people to look down into the alleys between Nutty Squirrel's block-long storage sheds and see there was a party going on. I also hoped that Bo the drummer knew a dentist who didn't ask a lot of personal questions, like the patient's name and address.

Anyway, as I told Lola, most of the arguing and intrigue was lost on Teresa, who doesn't understand much English. And when the Knuckleheads weren't arguing, the rehearsals were wonderful to hear. No more taking it from the top every three or four bars. Nobody had the heart to stop Teresa once she got going. The one time they tried—for technical reasons—she was so certain they were saying that the squealing of the speaker was somehow her fault

that she ran home and wouldn't come back. Bo the drummer had
to go after her, pleading, with a Spanish-English dictionary.

The Gig

Lola, who was out of the hospital in plenty of time for Knucklehead's first gig with Teresa and the Ramirez twins, showed up at
the Red Stallion in a Dale Evans blouse and string tie, with a silver belt buckle the size of a saucer on her blue jeans, a cowboy hat
on her head, and a pair of hand-tooled boots on her feet. She
taught me how to do the Texas Two-step, which is an actual dance,
I found, very similar to the fox trot. By the end of the night, I could
almost talk and dance at the same time.

"We're having a transcendent experience," she told me a little
breathlessly out on the floor.

"Where did *you* learn to dance like this?" I asked her, counting
one-two-THREE-four in my head.

"'The truths are few,'" she said, "'and available to all.'"

We had only one bad moment, during the first break, when a
drunk approached the table where Lola and I sat with Teresa, the
twins, and a couple of Knuckleheads. The drunk asked Teresa if she
knew "This Crazy Life." Teresa does, in fact, know the tune—it happened to be on the song list for the second set—but she didn't have
a clue as to what the guy leaning sloppily over the back of her chair
was saying to her. When the steel player answered for her, the guy
got mad, said he was talking to the lady, etc., etc., and before you
knew it, the twins were on their feet in defense of Teresa, and the
drummer was pulling the steel player away from the drunk. This is
it, I thought, this is it—but I was wrong, because all of a sudden it
was time for the second set and all Knucklehead personnel headed
for the stage. Couples and singles flooded the dance floor, a sizable
contingent of Nutty Squirrel residents among them. The second set
was even better than the first. Teresa sang "Walking after Midnight"
in a cloud of blue smoke. The drunk nursed his beer at the end of
the bar and left us alone for the rest of the night.

Lola was in the hospital again three weeks later, when the
Knuckleheads made their triumphant return to the Red Stallion.

(I went to visit her. She looked frail and groggy, said she was having trouble with headaches and couldn't sleep. She told me that only now could she really appreciate what Kneecha meant when Zarathustra says, "Blessed are the sleepy ones, for they shall soon drop off.") It was practically standing room only at the Stallion on Saturday night, but my heart wasn't in it without Lola to bully me around the dance floor, so I left before the third set, which is when Immigration and Naturalization showed up, responding to an anonymous tip from an irate citizen nursing a grudge at the bar.

Disconnected

Once I lived in a storage warehouse where a guy collected telephones. I don't know what he was up to, but his self-storage cubicle was a roomful of telephones, piled high in one corner and tumbling down on top of each other, with their cords all coiling and tangled from one to the next, so you wouldn't want to have to pick one of those phones and pull it out from the rest. Most of the telephones were old black models with dials instead of buttons. They were the kind of phone nobody wanted, colored wires sticking out of the bottoms of some of them, some of them upside down with the bottom plate off so you could see the bell.

When I was a kid, my father gave me an old phone like that for my very own. It was when they came out with princess phones in colors and my sister wanted a pink one to match the wallpaper in her room, so my father gave me her old one. One night at the supper table I complained about how nobody ever called me on my new phone, and my father explained that the phone wasn't *connected*. It was just to play with. My sister snickered.

After supper I went upstairs to see if I could make sense out of what my father had said. It wasn't connected, he said. I stared at the phone there on the table next to my bed, where it looked as if it might ring at any moment, although I'd given up that hope by now. I squatted down with my hands on my knees so that I'd be at eye level with the bedside table, expecting to see a space between the bottom of the telephone and the table top. It wasn't connected, he said. But he was wrong, because the telephone rested squarely on the table, and the table was connected to the table legs and the table legs went all the way to the floor and the floor came all the way over to my feet, which were connected to my legs, which were connected to my middle and all the rest. I got mad at the phone then for making a fool out of me and my father and, reaching out, I swept it off the table with my arm. When it hit the floor, that phone finally rang. The dial also popped off, as did a few other things, including the bottom plate, so I saw the bell. I saw that inside the phone there was an actual bell. It wasn't the phone that rang, it was the bell inside it. When I pointed this out to my father (who came upstairs to see what had fallen), he thought I was exhibiting curiosity about the inner workings of the telephone, so he screwed off both ends of the receiver to show me the colored wires and metal plates inside the smooth plastic place where you put your ear and the sprinkling-can part where you talk. Weeks went by before I could put a telephone receiver to my head again.

Every once in a while in the old storage place, from my own little cubicle there, usually in the dead of night when the traffic volume was turned down low, I would hear a jangle in Number Seven and I knew that a phone must have slid off the snake pile and hit the floor. At first I used to have to fight the impulse to jump up, calling, "I'll get it!" I can tell you that it takes practice to let a phone go ahead and ring if it wants to. You have to teach yourself not to respond.

I answered the phone today at the Nutty Squirrel office, which is to my knowledge the only telephone on the premises. It was somebody from Mercy Hospital. It seems Lola had asked them to call me. They told me that she died.

"Let's give these suckers a break."

Lola taught me a secret about people who rent self-storage cubicles. Secretly, they wish the warehouse where they've squirreled away their most precious commodities would burn to the ground, taking the goods with it. Secretly, they rue the fireproof walls, the concrete slab of a floor, the absence of careless smokers and overloaded circuits and extension cords hidden under the rug. Somewhere, deep down, they despise the goods—"*sic:* gods," Lola would say, her eyebrow aloft—that enslave them, the easy payment plans and plastic by which they are held in thrall.

Why else, she would ask, do we love the movies that stage the final fight scene in a mansion stuffed with objets-d'art, affording us the thrill of seeing gold-framed mirrors and stained-glass windows shattered, or the flawless polished surface of a dining table the size of a football field plowed with bullets? We all like to see the priceless vase knocked off its pedestal. We like to see the velvet upholstery and the leather—finer by far than the stuff we've scrimped and saved for, covering it with sheets to protect it from cats and children—slashed to shreds by a knife-wielding burglar. Most of all, we like the chase scenes that demolish not a Ford or a Toyota, but a Jaguar, a Mercedes, a Porsche. Maybe several.

Thus do we take our vicarious revenge against the goods for which we daily traipse to our deadening jobs, Lola always said, we who owe our souls to MasterCard and BankOne Visa.

"Kneecha puts it this way," she said one night, brandishing a copy of *The Will to Power*. "'Man finds himself in those goods which are his because he has previously lost himself in them.'"

"You can say that again," I said.

So Lola said, "'Where a man's treasure lies, there lies his heart also.'"

"That's not Kneecha," I said.

"No, it isn't."

Lola, who was not feeling great at the time, had stood up then and dropped the book on the seat of her Queen Anne chair. She shivered and hugged herself for warmth. "Maybe we should torch the place," she said. "Give these suckers a break."

"I speak on behalf of orphaned things."

All in all, the INS raid at the Red Stallion pretty much decimated our migrant population. Those who weren't actually picked up at the bar were warned by a couple of teenagers who were out in the steel player's pickup having an illegal drink when the blue vans arrived. They escaped on foot and sounded the alarm for the sleeping grandmothers and kids back here. They could have stayed, as it turned out. Nobody blew the whistle on Nutty Squirrel.

I was fitting my stuff into a small U-Haul truck—the same U-Haul I'd used to bring back enough gasoline (secured by the gallon at a half-dozen different stations) to send the orphaned goods of Nutty Squirrel wafting in billows of smoke to the sky—when I heard tires on gravel. Somebody had pulled into the parking lot in front of the office. If it was the INS, no problem; there were no migrants, legal or otherwise, on the premises. If it was my boss, Mr. Nutty Squirrel, then I could only hope he wouldn't take a peek into One West and spot my little stockpile of red gasoline cans. If it was a renter come to visit his or her goods, well, I was in no hurry. I'd give them time to say good-bye.

When I poked my head out the back of the trailer, I saw Bo the Knucklehead drummer opening the passenger side of his station wagon. He had Teresa with him. When she saw me, she smiled with her new white teeth and came dancing my way, uncertain on the gravel in the high-heeled boots they had bought her for the gig. I hopped out of the trailer and closed the door on the gasoline cans in One West.

"Buenas, buenas!" she cried when she reached me, throwing her arms around me and taxing my Spanish to the fullest with a steady stream of history—where they had taken her mother and the Ramirez twins and all the others, how Señor the Drummer Bo had come to bail them out, how they had a plan (here she looked shyly at the drummer) to keep her in the United States, how they were going to get work permits for her and the twins to tour with the band, how they all had me to thank for their good fortune. She still smelled like smoke from the Stallion; I know I smelled like gasoline. Bo the drummer came out of 9W with some Knucklehead equipment that he dumped in the back of the wagon before he came clomping over. (Never saw a man so awkward in cowboy boots as Bo the Knucklehead drummer.) He filled me in on the parts of the story I'd lost in the translation. He thanked me, too. I was glad that the band liked to haul every piece of equipment to every gig. Now that he had come back for that soundboard thing, their cubicle was empty except for a broken mike stand and some knotted extension cords. He put

his arm around Teresa on the way back to the station wagon and hollered *"Vaya con Dios!"* to me out the window as they drove away. I could see her laughing at him in the passenger seat.

The visit from Teresa and Bo the drummer only renewed my resolve to give the rest of these suckers a break. In fact, I had a book of matches in my hand when the ups truck pulled into the parking lot. The guy had me sign for a cardboard box, unmarked except for my name and the Nutty Squirrel address. It wasn't heavy. I waited until he left before I opened it and found a brass canister about the size of a two-pound coffee can. The top of the can bore the inscription, nicely embossed in the brass:

> Lola Valorian
> 1959–1996
> "a thing among things"
> Independent Mortuary Service
> Cedar Rapids

In the box with the canister was a brown envelope full of other envelopes and papers—copies of Lola's birth certificate, her driver's license (already cut in half), her library card (left whole), and a life insurance policy with the original beneficiaries crossed out (the word *deceased* handwritten above them) and my name penned in their place, all of it duly notarized at the bottoms of the pages.

After I went through the envelope, I said, "Hey, Lola." Maybe I cried a little. It didn't matter, since nobody was there to see, although it probably goes to show that I'm not autistic.

So all of a sudden there I was with a room full of gasoline and a can full of ashes, and it's up to me what comes next. In the end, if you want to call it that, I put her life insurance into escrow to pay thirty-five dollars a month—adjustable as storage fees increase—for the next 124 years or so. The country band—renamed *Teresa's Dynamite Ranch*—recorded a song that made it to the Country Top Forty and then the band sort of fell out of sight, although they might be playing nightly in Branson, Missouri, for all I know. I bought one of their tapes just to hear the sound of Teresa's voice, but I haven't listened to it yet. By the time Mr. Nutty Squirrel found the gallons of gasoline in One West, I'd moved across town to Grandma's

Attic, an old brick brewery building divided into eight-by-tens. I rent a third-floor unit with a window. Two old ladies live in the unit right below mine. Sometimes I hear them laughing at night. Once a week I go to visit Lola where she rests like Tut, arrayed in brass on her wing chair and surrounded by her orphaned things, under the sign of the fetus, under the sign of the hoarding squirrel. Mummy or dummy, I always tell her, take your pick. It's a whole new world in here.

On the Coast
of Bohemia

Lucy Kopecky escaped from the After School Program at Herbert Hoover Elementary during the brief interval between Story Hour, which ended the regular school day, and Snack Time, which marked the start of After School. She had no trouble escaping. All she had to do was replace herself in the ranks with Jennifer Collins, another fourth-grader who had always longed to join her friends After School but had a mother at home around the corner and thus did not qualify for the program. The other kids went along with what Lucy called the old switcheroo because, as she later explained to Helen, "Jenny's cool. I'm not."

"Is that your way of saying that the others prefer Jennifer's company to yours?"

"Afraid so," said Lucy.

Helen stirred indignantly in her rocking chair. She straightened her shoulders, tilted her head—endangering a baseball cap that teetered on her snowy hair—then lifted her hands off the top of the cane she held between her knees and clapped them back down again. Lucy immediately recognized this series of movements as *bristling*, a word she had often come across in her reading but had previously understood only in the vaguest way. Bristling, Helen said,

"And these children are so rude as to make their preference known to you?"

Lucy shrugged. "They're not hostile to me. They just ignore me. That's how I know."

Lucy had met Helen for the first time only moments after sliding down the hill behind Herbert Hoover to the gap in the chain link fence, and squeezing through it into the cemetery, where she dodged headstones deftly and gave a wide berth to the kind of monuments she thought of as little houses of the dead. When Lucy emerged from the cemetery on Dewey Street, she found herself face to façade with a house she had often admired while pedaling down Dewey to enjoy the way the cobblestones made her handlebars tickle the palms of her hands. It was directly across the street from the iron gates of the cemetery: a green frame house of many gables, nooks, and crannies, surrounded in early September by last stands of snapdragons, hollyhocks, and mums. The Victorian flagship of the block. Lucy already knew that someone interesting lived there. Once, as she rode past, she had seen the front door open slightly and a thin, white arm thrust through the crack, strewing bread crusts on the porch like confetti. Before the arm withdrew, squirrels began to gather.

From the other side of the street, Lucy noticed next to the porch of the green frame house a juniper bush with at least a dozen rolled-up *Advertisers* sticking out of the branches. Feeling that anyone considerate enough to feed the squirrels deserved a newspaper carrier with better aim than that, and looking for something to do until five o'clock, when her mother expected to pick her up at Hoover After School, Lucy crossed the street. She collected an armful of *Advertisers* and carried them to the front porch but got only as far as the middle of the steps before an old woman appeared behind the screen door, crying, "Don't take another step!"

Lucy froze. After several moments of awkward silence, she slowly raised one of the newspapers in her hand, so the woman could see what it was, but she had no sooner moved her arm than the old woman cried, more urgently than before, *"Don't move!"*

Lucy froze again. She tried to remember if she had heard anything about the woman who lived in the green house, whether she was supposed to be senile or murderous. From what Lucy could see of her through the screen, she looked like a normal white-haired lady, except perhaps for the baseball cap. When she spoke again, her voice was calm and measured, as if she were giving Lucy instructions for a party game. "Keep your hands at your sides," she said, "and move one baby step to the right."

Surprised at her own willingness to obey, Lucy took one baby step to the right.

"Now one more—just a *hair* toward me. Just a hair."

Lucy moved forward a hair.

"Can you see it now?" the old woman said, beaming at the empty air between them.

"See what?" said Lucy.

"Oh, dear." The old woman's smile faded. "If I could only come out and position you properly—but of course I can't open the door. Try taking one teeny, tiny step back to the left and look again."

Lucy took the teeniest, tiniest of steps to the left and said, "But what am I supposed to see?—Oh! Oh, *look*."

Stretched across the air in front of her, from the porch pillar on her left to the corner of the screen door and back to the porch pillar on her right, a shimmering net billowed out into the sunlight and fell back into the shade. It was an orb web of the utmost magnificence, the fine silk threads invisible in shadow but silver in the light.

"Spiders are such cunning creatures," the old woman said.

"They do beautiful work," Lucy agreed.

*　　*　　*

They sat on the back porch of the green house for more than an hour that first afternoon, Helen straight-backed in the wooden rocker, her hands resting on the top of her four-footed metal cane, and Lucy on the steps, twirling a lock of long brown ponytail as she described for Helen the After School Program's grueling schedule of nonstop activities. Kickball. Nature Corner. Snack Time. Arts & Crafts.

"What if you want to read a book?" Helen asked her.

"You're out of luck," said Lucy.

"No wonder you had to get out."

Helen said that if you substituted Book Talk for Kickball, After School sounded a lot like the last retirement home her son Walter had taken her to see. She told Lucy (as she had told Walter many times) that it was crazy the way people were shut up all day in their little compartments, sorted according to age rather than temperament or taste or mutual interests. "No wonder people are lonely," she said. "No wonder they're bored. Take you and me, for instance. Why should the mere fact that I'm a little older than you are keep us from enjoying one another's company?" She would be eighty-four in December, Helen confided. Lucy admitted to going on ten, quickly adding that she had always gotten along better with adults than with people her own age. "I read a lot," Lucy said. "My mother says I prefer adults because of my expansive vocabulary."

"No doubt," Helen said expansively.

"My sister says it's because I'm a geek."

"Your sister is obviously in possession of a vocabulary as limited as it is crude. Not to mention inaccurate."

"You said it," said Lucy.

It took two weeks of sitting side by side with Helen on her porch swing, watching squirrels dart up the steps to stuff their cheeks with bread, before Lucy overcame a lifetime of warnings against entering the home of a stranger and finally went inside the green house on Dewey Street one cold and rainy afternoon in late September. She stood dripping on the hardwood floor of the front hall while Helen rubbed her head with a towel and lectured her on the importance of wearing a hat. "My mother used to say, if your hands or feet are cold, put on a hat. The body can't worry about appendages when it's busy keeping your brain warm. That's why I wear one all the time." Today it was a close-fitting cloth cap brilliantly embroidered with flowers. "Mayan," Helen said when Lucy admired it. "From the Yucatan." While Helen rubbed, Lucy sniffed the sweet, slightly ripe smell of the house, a blend of mustiness, wood polish, Spic'n'Span, and a hint of something sharp and nutty that she could not identify. "It's the squirrels," Helen explained. "They're in the attic." She looked down at Lucy's sodden tennis shoes. "I'm afraid I have to ask you to remove your sneakers, if you don't mind. My son has his eye on the rug in the library. It's a genuine Sirhouk."

Shoeless, Lucy followed Helen through the arched doorway on their left into a darkened room that had a smell of its own—at once familiar and oddly out of place. While Helen went to the window, Lucy wiggled her toes in the thick pile of an Oriental carpet whose ornate border was barely visible in the gloom. In a moment, the blinds squeaked open, striping the room with light. Under Lucy's feet, the genuine Sirhouk bloomed in dark red and gold. "I keep the blinds closed so the sunlight won't damage the leather bindings," Helen said as she moved to another window, "but I don't think we need to worry about sunlight on a day like today, do we?" She turned around to look at Lucy. "Are you still with me? Is something wrong?"

"I've just never seen so many books in somebody's actual house before," Lucy said.

"Well, come in and take a closer look," said Helen. Leaving her metal cane at the window, she carefully crossed the wine-colored rug to a wall covered with books from floor to ceiling. "My husband and I taught at the university many years ago," Helen said, "back when it was called the Teacher's College." She ran her hand along the spines on the nearest shelf and laughed. "Clifford was the whole Classics Department. I was Medieval and Renaissance Literature—until our son Walter came along, that is. In those days, *that* was the end of that." She brushed the bookshelf dust from her palms. "Some of these books are quite rare and valuable. Like the red ones behind you. Plutarch. In Greek, of course."

Lucy turned around to look at a shelf of slim red volumes, their indecipherable titles etched in gold marks on the spines, a code waiting to be cracked.

"I'm leaving them all to the university in my will," Helen was saying. "They'll put them in the rare books collection, in a room named after my husband and me. My son even brought the librarian or curator or whatever he was over here to work on preserving the books from termites and weevils and so on. I thought that was a little insensitive of Walter, to tell you the truth. I'm not dead yet."

Lucy continued her slow pirouette in the middle of the rug. "You sure are lucky to have all these books to read," she said.

"The only problem is, I can't read them."

Lucy stopped. "You can't read?"

"Of course I can *read*," Helen said. "My eyes have gone bad. I can't see to read anymore."

Lucy peered at Helen's face. "Can't you get glasses? I had glasses in second grade, but then my eyes changed or something so I didn't need them."

"I'm afraid glasses don't help when you have cataracts. Mine make a hole in the middle of my field of vision. It's pretty hard to read when all you can see are the words around the edges."

"Isn't there something you can do to fix it?" Lucy looked at the wall of books. How could anyone stand to have so many and not be able to read them?

"Surgery," Helen said, "but I'm too old for an operation."

"Are you sure? My grandpa had an operation when he was very old. On his heart."

"Trust me. I'm too old. And this is a dreary subject. Have you found something interesting there?"

Lucy blew the dust from a set of four thick blue bindings. "Shakespeare!" she said.

"You like Shakespeare, do you?"

"My mother took a course in him once. She used to read to us at night. To put us to sleep."

"Your mother sounds like a clever woman."

"I think she read us *A Winter's Tale*."

"Volume Two," said Helen. "Why don't you take it down and we'll have a look." While Lucy struggled to pull the heavy book out from between its fellows, Helen sat down in the larger of two leather chairs that stood, with a little table between them, on an island of protective plastic in the middle of the genuine Sirhouk. ("Mother's Day gift from my son Walter," Helen explained, tapping the hard plastic with the heel of her thick black shoe.) She took the book Lucy offered her and laid it open across her lap. "You know," she said, turning the pages without looking at them, "they tell you that Shakespeare knows everything about love and war and history, about what makes men and women do cruel things to each other. Shakespeare was a genius—that's what they tell you in school, right?"

"Well," said Lucy. "We really haven't done that much Shake-speare yet."

"I'm going to show you something about Shakespeare," Helen said. She had reached a page marked by a red ribbon and pointed to a passage with her gnarly finger. "See this? You read it. Here."

"I don't think I can read *Shakespeare*," Lucy said.

"For heaven's sake, why not?" said Helen, motioning her into the other chair. "Start right here."

Lucy took the book in both hands. It was wonderfully heavy, the pages lay flat, and ribbon markers flowed from the top and bottom like streamers. The print was much bigger than the tiny type she remembered in her mother's *Complete Works;* these words, though strange, looked almost readable. "'Thou didst speak but well,'" she began slowly, one word at a time.

Helen interrupted. "Farther down. After the space. Scene III."

Lucy cleared her throat and began again. "'Scene III,'" she read. "'Bohemia. A desert country near the sea.'"

"Ha!" said Helen.

"What?" said Lucy.

"Go on."

Lucy hesitated.

"'Enter Antigonus,'" Helen prompted.

"'Enter Antigonus, with the Babe, and a Mariner,'" said Lucy. She frowned at the page. "I know this part. This is where they leave the baby on the shore to die. That king was a jerk. He locks his wife up, lets one kid die of sadness, leaves the baby to the wolves, and then his wife goes back to him in the end? How can that be a happy ending?" When her mother read the play, Lucy had secretly cried herself to sleep over the fate of the little prince who wasted away with longing for his mother.

"That's Shakespeare for you," said Helen. "But read what Antigonus says. Right after 'Thou art perfect then.'"

"Okay. Let's see. Here. 'Thou art perfect then, our ship hath touch'd upon the deserts of Bohemia.'"

"Ha," Helen said again. "That's enough." She folded her arms across her chest. "What did I tell you about Mr. Shakespeare?"

Lucy looked down at the book in her lap and re-read the lines to herself. "I don't get it," she said. "What's wrong with that?"

Helen unfolded her arms. "What's *wrong* with it?"

"Don't they have deserts in Bohemia?"

"Don't they have—well, no, they don't, not if you mean deserts full of sand, but that's probably not what he means. In Shakespeare's day, *deserts* meant wild places, wilderness. Bohemia had plenty of wilderness back then, I'm sure, but I'll tell you what it didn't have then and doesn't have now." She paused. Lucy waited. "It doesn't have a coast!"

Lucy looked the passage over one more time. "Oh!" she said. "I get it. How can a *ship* come to rest if there isn't any coast?"

"Exactly." Helen looked pleased. "Shakespeare's geography was terrible," she said.

*   *   *

That night, Lucy sat up in bed with a circle of black construction paper about three inches wide in front of the book she was trying to read. She jumped when her mother came in and asked, "What are you doing?"

"Nothing," Lucy said, shoving the black circle into the book.

"An experiment for science?" her mother tried.

"That's right!" said Lucy. "We're learning about cat-something."

"Cataracts?"

"That's it. They make a hole in the middle of the page you're reading. Like this." She pulled the black circle out of the book and held it over the page. "It's terrible. How can you read with a hole in the page?"

"I think they can operate to remove cataracts," her mother said.

"Yeah," Lucy said sadly, going back to her book. "But some people are too old for surgery."

The next day, however, as she watched the boldest of the squirrels—a fat one Helen called Falstaff—sidle up to the porch swing and snatch a crust of bread right out of Helen's hand, Lucy was struck by a brilliant idea.

"What if I read *to* you?" she said. "I'm a really good reader. I read while I'm walking and I take books to pajama parties so my sister says it's no wonder nobody invites me to come anymore, but it just goes to show—I have a lot of reading experience. Last time I tested I was way, way ahead of my grade. That's what really bugs my sister, if you want to know the truth."

"The truth is usually relative, Lucy," Helen said, but she was smiling a little.

"Not that Clare is stupid—she's not—but when it comes to reading, I can't be beat. My teacher Mrs. Cilek says—"

"Enough of your resumé!" Helen said, laughing. "I don't require references. Let's go upstairs and I'll put you to work."

"Upstairs?" said Lucy.

"That's where I keep the really good stuff."

Going upstairs was a painstaking process that involved waiting on each step while Helen hauled herself and her four-legged cane up to the next tread.

"You need one of those elevator chairs where you sit and ride up along the railing," Lucy said at her friend's elbow.

"I need a new pair of knees," Helen puffed.

It was worth the long haul. Boxes of books lined walls papered with hunting dogs and ivy in her son Walter's former bedroom, and in those boxes, under layers of novels whose pages were gray with tiny print, Lucy found *Alice in Wonderland, Wind in the Willows,* a complete set of Narnia *Chronicles,* and even lesser known greats like *The Borrowers—Afield, Afloat,* and *Aloft.* She exclaimed over each one as she pulled them from the box. Helen sat on the edge of her son's former bed, watching.

"Some of these were my books and some were Wally's," she explained, "and some were books I bought but somehow never managed to send along as presents for—oh, for nieces or nephews, maybe even for the grandchildren I used to think I might have."

"My Side of the Mountain!" Lucy cried. "I love this book!"

"Now that would be Wally's," Helen said. "I remember buying it for him the first time he went to camp." She thought for a moment. "He was nine years old, like you."

"I read it when I was six," Lucy said.

"I'm not surprised."

Lucy had moved on to another box. "Who's this?" she said and held up a framed photograph of a bride and groom—she a startling, dark-haired beauty in a narrow dress and long veil, he a stern young man seated in his morning coat, balancing a top hat on his knee. The bride stood with her hand on the groom's shoulder, and, in spite of the stiffness of the pose, a little smile softened the corners of her mouth.

"Who do you think?" said Helen.

Lucy looked up at Helen, then down at the picture, then back at Helen. "It's you!"

"You needn't sound quite so surprised, dear."

"You were *beautiful*," Lucy said.

"Thank you. I think."

Lucy took notice of Helen's tone. "I like the way you are now better," she said gallantly.

"Baloney," said Helen.

"I mean it," Lucy said. "You look better with white hair."

"Sliced thicker and thicker," said Helen.

"And this is your husband," Lucy said, settling back on her heels and resting the edge of the frame on her knees.

"A reasonable deduction," said Helen.

"Tell me about him," Lucy said. "What was he like?"

Helen pursed her lips, as though she were choosing from a long menu of attributes. "Cliff made me laugh," she said finally. "He was a little absentminded, like the professor in the cliché, but he was a good teacher, very popular—no small feat, for a classicist. Most important," and here she leaned toward Lucy for emphasis, "he was a good dancer. The man *liked* to dance."

"Why is that so important?"

"Wait a few years, Lucy. You won't have to ask." Helen reached down for the photograph. Lucy handed it to her. "He was a good husband and a good friend," Helen said. "I guess in some ways it was fortunate that he died pretty young, before I got too attached to him."

Lucy was shocked. "What do you mean?" she said.

Helen touched the face of the young man in the photograph, caressing the glass with her finger. "The truth is, Lucy, if you live with them too long, you lose yourself. It's so easy to rely on somebody else like that—and not just for fixing faucets and putting up storm windows, either. Pretty soon you forget who you are—or who you used to be." She shook her head. "I've seen it happen again and again. To my sisters, to my friends. The old man passes away after all those years together, and the old lady has nothing left. Now when Clifford died, I was not so far gone. I could still imagine myself without him."

"How old was he?" Lucy asked. "When he died, I mean."

Helen set the picture on the bed beside her. "Sixty-seven," she said with a sigh.

Lucy pulled other photographs from the box—picnickers at the beach, an apple-cheeked boy with an enormous Easter basket, the groom and the bride looking older and younger in a variety of places and poses. "Why do you keep your pictures up here where nobody sees them?" she asked Helen.

"Well, that's another issue. I'll tell you. People my age have trouble remembering things, everyday things, but they can remember the past as if it happened yesterday. Do you know why? Because the past is the only time they believe in. They surround themselves with it. They cover every wall with it. They clutter up the top of the piano. They're so occupied with what they think they've lost that they can't pick up anything new. I don't want to be like that."

"I wonder if my grandma has ever thought of that," said Lucy. "She loses her car keys at least once a week, and she's got pictures everywhere."

"You might talk with her about it sometime, Lucy. Tell her you can only hold so much. Tell her if your hands are full of the past, it's hard to keep a hold of the present."

*   *   *

They started their reading with *Alice in Wonderland* and *Through the Looking Glass*. By Lewis Carroll. (Helen always made Lucy read the complete title and the author's name. "Give credit where it's due," Helen said.) She sat on her son's bed and gazed out the window at the changing leaves of an oak tree in front of the house, while Lucy sat on the floor and read, the words creating worlds around them in the usual, miraculous way. By the wildest of uncoincidences, *Alice* happened to be not only Lucy's "all-time favorite book on the planet" but Helen's as well. "I read it over and over," Helen told Lucy, "so many times that my mother took it away from me. I must have been seven or eight years old. She told me to read something else for a while. I was devastated, until one night, lying in bed, I realized that I had all the scenes in my head and I could go through them from beginning to end, whenever I pleased, just as if I were reading them." Helen looked thoughtful. "It was a revelation for me, Lucy, knowing that no one—not even my mother—could take what I had read away from me."

"And she couldn't stop you from thinking about it either," said Lucy, who had discovered during one of her sister's dance recitals the astounding fact, both lonely and liberating, that no one else—not even her mother—could tell what she was really thinking.

With time off for feeding squirrels and taking tea in the library (carefully restricting liquids and sticky pastries to the island of plastic), Lucy and Helen spent more than a week's worth of afternoons making their way *Through the Looking Glass.* Near the end, when Alice reached the Eighth Square, they set the book aside and did most of the chapter from memory, with Lucy as the White Queen, Helen as the Red, and Wally's old GI Joe doll, on a folding chair between them, as Alice. Lucy and Helen kept silent for GI Joe's part. Each of them heard Alice in her head.

*   *   *

It couldn't last forever; they both knew that. The very calendar was against them, days growing shorter as September wore on into October, so that Lucy had to leave a little earlier each week. Helen always stood on the porch and watched her go, straining against the fading light to follow the pink or yellow sweatshirt and swinging ponytail through the yard across the street and into the dusky stretch of graveyard behind it as Lucy raced the sunset back to school. There she joined stragglers on the playground or lurked outside the entrance until her mother's car showed up at five o'clock. It was only a matter of time, they knew, before darkness overtook her, or the After School staff made a shocking discovery, or Helen's son Walter demanded to meet the new friend whose name his mother had let slip one evening when Walter came by with her dinner.

"He thinks you're a white-haired old lady," she told Lucy, chuckling.

"Is that what you told him?"

"What—lie to my own son? No sir, I didn't say a word about your date of birth. He made his own assumptions."

"Would he care if he knew I was a kid?"

"Oh my, yes. He'd look into who you are and where you live and whether your parents are likely to file a lawsuit against me if you fall down the stairs or get bitten by a squirrel. Walter has always been terribly afraid of getting sued. It's an occupational hazard with lawyers, I think. If you really want to get his dander up, just say: *So sue me*. He turns purple."

Lucy was alone in the library one afternoon in mid-October, setting the little table for tea, when a sudden banging on the front door startled her so much that she knocked over the sugar bowl, causing a small, white avalanche from the table to the plastic under her feet. Frantically sweeping it up with a bookmark and her own personal copy of *The Secret Garden*, she was horrified to hear the front door creaking open, followed by heavy footsteps in the hall and a deep voice calling, "Mother?"

There was no place to hide. A thin, balding man who did not in the least resemble the apple-cheeked boy in the photos upstairs was already standing in the arched doorway of the library, the toes of his wing tips nudging the rug. "What are you doing in here?" he said, too shocked, apparently, to bother with hello. Lucy did her best to explain herself. She was rescued by Helen's voice floating out to them from her room on the far side of the hallway, faint but clear, asking her son to come here for a moment, please. Walter looked at Lucy.

"I was just going outside," she said tactfully. Out on the porch, she heard the lock click behind her and then, coming from the window of Helen's room, the rise and fall of voices vying for the last word. She made out "Lucy" once—that was Helen—but mostly it was Walter saying words like "some kid," "damn squirrels," and, *"Mother!"* Then silence fell. Before long, Walter came down the driveway from the back of the house, got into his car, and drove away without so much as a glance at the front porch, where Lucy had been standing so still in the shadows that squirrels had gathered hopefully at her feet. They ran off scolding when Helen opened the door. She apologized breathlessly for her son's behavior and they went on with their preparations for tea—"Sirhouk be damned!" said Helen—but the teacups she picked up chattered so loudly in their saucers that Lucy had to take them from her and ask her what was wrong.

Helen folded her hands in her lap. "Lucy," she said, "what would you say if I told you that we can't go on meeting this way?"

"Whoa," said Lucy. "I'd say your son was pretty mad about finding a kid in the library."

"He was—concerned," Helen admitted.

"About the rug?"

Helen smiled. "Oh, my son is concerned about so many things," she said. "The rug, the squirrels, his doddering old mother. I'm very vulnerable, you know. You could crack my skull and stuff your pockets with rare books or roll up the Sirhouk and hide it under your shirt. And even if you wouldn't, even if you're a nice, normal kid—although what kind of nice, normal nine year old would befriend an old relic like me?—there's still the potential lawsuit to worry about." She lifted the teapot with a trembling hand and set it down again. "Would you mind?" Lucy took the teapot, and while she poured the first cup, Helen asked, "Did you tell him your name—your full name, I mean?"

"I think so—yes. Yes, I did." Lucy poured the second cup without a drip and put the teapot back in the cozy.

"And your address?"

"Just the street—oh no!" Lucy covered her mouth with her hand. "Do you think he'll call my mother?"

"He might."

"But then she'll know I haven't been to After School for *ages!*"

Helen looked into her teacup and said, "Maybe it's time she knew anyway."

"But, Helen—"

"All I mean," Helen said, "is that the longer you come here illegally, so to speak, the more likely it will seem that I conspired to bring you."

"What do you mean, conspired?" said Lucy.

"I mean conspired as in *conspiracy.*"

"You mean you could get in trouble because I skipped out?"

"With my son on the case," Helen said wryly, "I wouldn't rule out kidnapping charges." She frowned. "I wonder if he checked the attic before he left. If he did, he knows I sent his exterminator packing."

"Helen!" Lucy said. "Do you mean you could go to jail?"

"No such luck." Helen sipped her tea. "It'll be Oakview Manor for me."

"They'll put you in a nursing home?"

"A residential care facility," Helen corrected. "Oh, I don't know, Lucy. If I didn't want to go, I suppose he'd have to prove my incompetence first."

"But you're not incompetent. You're smarter than Shakespeare!"

Helen shrugged. "What good does that do me if I've got Squirrel City in my attic?"

*   *   *

They didn't need Walter to blow the whistle on them, though. Lucy did it herself, with a little help from William Shakespeare, in the final round of the district geography bee, fourth-grade division. They were well into Alphabet Soup, a new event this year, when Mr. Ploof, the moderator, asked Lucy's team for a landlocked nation whose name begins with the letter B. Lucy's hand shot up—along with those of teammates Matt Gerber and Ben Price—and when Mr. Ploof called on Lucy, she stood up and said, without the slightest hesitation in her loud, clear voice, "Bohemia!" There followed a chorus of exclamations from the gallery—where Lucy's mother and sister Clare sat watching—and a strangled groan from Matt Gerber, who had been thinking, of course, of Bolivia, Botswana, or any of a half-dozen obvious B's, all of them landlocked. When the judges, after consulting their maps and rule books, disallowed "Bohemia" for having disappeared from the map in 1918, the question went to the competing team, which promptly offered Burkina Faso and walked away with the district championship, fourth-grade division. Defeat would have been bad enough if Matt Gerber—a passionate overachiever—hadn't stood up to insult Lucy and then knock the glasses off teammate Ben Price, who had risen in her defense. As Ben's glasses hit the floor, Lucy's arm swung up from her side like a pendulum ("You *hit* him, Lucy?" Helen asked later) and her fist caught Matt Gerber under the chin. ("A bitten tongue bleeds like crazy," Lucy told Helen. "They almost called an ambulance.")

In the car on the way home, Lucy's sister carried on as if she would never be able to hold her head up in public again. "Why couldn't you say something normal," she moaned, "like Britain or Brazil?"

"Those places aren't landlocked," said Lucy.

Lucy's mother told Clare to keep still. Then she asked Lucy, "Why Bohemia?"

"It's landlocked," Lucy said. "It starts with a B."

"Yes," her mother said, "but why *Bohemia?*"

"It's from Shakespeare," Lucy said and immediately wished she hadn't.

"Shakespeare," her mother said. "Are you studying one of his plays at school?"

"Are you kidding, Mom?" said Clare. "They don't study Shakespeare in fourth grade. How much do you want to bet she got this Shakespeare stuff from one of her weird friends?"

"I don't have weird friends," said Lucy.

"It's that old bald lady, isn't? In the green house on Dewey."

"What are you talking about?" Lucy said. "Helen isn't bald."

"Then how come she's always wearing a dumb hat?"

"She's keeping her brain warm—which is something *you* wouldn't have to worry about!"

"Wait a minute!" their mother cried. "Who is Helen?"

Lucy folded her arms across her chest. "Helen is my friend."

*   *   *

There was a big to-do when Lucy's two-month truancy from the After School Program was discovered. If Lucy had been a little older and wiser—or if she'd had a chance to talk things over with Helen—she would have understood that it was only guilt and fear at having lost track of her daughter so easily and for so long that led Lucy's mother to declare the green frame house on Dewey Street strictly off limits. Lucy protested.

"I can't just never show up at Helen's again. She'll worry that something *terrible* happened to me."

"You weren't so concerned about *my* worrying, were you?" said her mother. (As Helen would explain later to Lucy, there was probably a little maternal jealousy at work here as well.)

"But you weren't worried," Lucy said. "You didn't even *know* I wasn't where you thought I was."

"I know now," her mother said.

Lucy tried another tack. "Don't you even want to meet Helen?"

"Maybe I do," said her mother. "Maybe I do."

A half-dozen squirrels darted nervously up and down the steps as Lucy and her mother rang the bell and waited at Helen's front door on the Monday after the geography bee. The porch, Lucy noticed, was curiously clean-swept. "It takes Helen kind of a long time to get to the door," she explained, ringing the bell a second time. Her finger had barely left the button when the door opened and Helen's son Walter frowned at them—or perhaps he only looked at them sadly—through the screen.

Lucy had to concentrate to make her legs walk past the door that Walter held open. Inside, she was so shocked to see that the leather chairs in the library had been pushed to one side and the genuine Sirhouk rolled up and covered in plastic, that she hardly heard the somber introductions, the apologies, the sad news that Helen had tripped and fallen in the library. "At her age," Walter was saying, "with a broken hip, she's—I'm afraid there's not much they can do." He pulled an envelope from the pocket of his jacket and held it out to Lucy. "She wanted me to give this to you."

Lucy took the envelope carefully from his hand, as if it might crumble when she touched it. The outside bore her name in wobbly letters. Inside, in different handwriting, as if she'd had someone write it for her, was a note:

> Dear Lucy,
>
> I forgot the most important thing in life:
> Always watch where you're going.
> Please feed the squirrels.
>
> > Your friend,
> > Helen

Lucy kept the note open in her lap in the car on the way to the hospital. At stoplights her mother heard her reading it under her breath like a spell or a prayer. After they found the wing and floor that Walter had written on the back of the envelope, Lucy's mother agreed to wait at the nurses' station for five full minutes while Lucy went down the hall to Helen's room alone. Lucy's mother watched her go—the untied tennis shoes taking careful steps, the ponytail swinging slowly—and when the time was up, she set off herself, far more reluctantly than her daughter had, to face the old woman's suffering and Lucy's grief. She was halfway down the hall before she heard the noises coming from Helen's room—noises so surprising that she had to pause outside the door and be sure of what she heard before she pushed it open.

They were laughing at something, Lucy hanging over the bed's metal side rail, giggling, while in the bed, a frail-looking woman chuckled carefully, holding her side, her skin nearly as white as the pillowcase she was wearing like a nightcap. They both looked up when the door opened.

"It's my mom!" said Lucy.

Helen's hand felt for the pillowcase on her head. "Oh dear," she said breathlessly, "I know I must look ridiculous, but you see, my feet were cold."

"She left her hat at home," Lucy added, and they broke up again into laughter that swept past Lucy's mother and escaped into the hall.

Stepping into the
World of Men

On April 26—three days before my wife was leaving without us
for unpronounceable cities like Ljubljana and Tržič—after six
seasons of bearing nothing but leaves, my peach trees burst into
bloom. Sweet-smelling blossoms, white, with the faintest blush of
pink at the center. So many you could hardly see the leaves.

When Madeline came downstairs that morning, I led her to the
back porch were I'd laid out breakfast facing the explosion of peach
blossoms, one small but loaded branch blooming strategically in a
jar near her plate.

"They're lovely," she said, meaning, *You just don't know when to
quit, do you?*

"They're a miracle," I said, meaning, *Even Mother Nature says:*
STAY HOME.

* * *

Two years ago Madeline was answering telephones part-time; now
she's got an inside-track, upper-management position in a biomedical supply company about to establish relations with what they call
their sister company in Slovenia. For the past nine months,
Madeline has been studying Intensive Slovenian (which, she tells

me, as if this should be somehow reassuring, is remarkably similar to Intensive Serbo-Croat), sticking signs and labels all over the house. *"Omarica,"* says the cupboard; *"sladkor,"* says the sugar bowl; *"kopalnica,"* says the bathroom door. My daughters—even little Lauren, who's only five—sweetly whisper, *"Lahko noč,* Daddy," when I go in to kiss them goodnight. As for me, I can't pronounce the names of half the places Madeline wants to drag us off to—and I don't believe for a minute that it's only for the summer. Already they're hinting around about the exceptional opportunities overseas for English-speaking biology teachers like me. *Whom* are they trying to kid? "Next thing you know," I told Madeline, "they'll be talking about permanent dislocation."

She laughed. "Don't you mean *re*location?"

"For you, maybe."

I didn't want to go to Slovenia even before my peach trees bloomed. I made a to-do list of things that I couldn't put off for another summer—hornets in the attic, crumbling concrete steps out front, the course syllabus I should have overhauled semesters ago. But Madeline wasn't impressed. "Get serious," she said.

When my son asked me to sign him up for Little League, I figured that was about as serious as we could get. Jeff was eleven, and he'd never played a game of fast-pitch hardball in his life, but he didn't want to go to Slovenia either. What if there were no video arcades in Ljubljana? no frog ponds in Tržič?

"But baseball!" my wife exclaimed when I told her. She was already packing her bags then, weeks in advance. "You hate baseball."

"I don't *hate* baseball."

She was folding my favorite blue sweater of hers. "He doesn't know the rules," she said. "He doesn't even know the positions."

"I've been making him some diagrams."

"Diagrams?" she said, as she put the blue sweater into the alarmingly large suitcase that lay open on the bed between us. She straightened up, pushing her bangs from her forehead in exactly the same way she'd been pushing them for the fifteen years I'd known her, and combing her fingers through to the blunt ends of a new haircut that was supposed to be businesslike and practical for travel but instead made her look—at least to my eyes—about seventeen. She said, "You'd better take him to the park and throw him a few."

She wanted to ask me again, I knew, if I'd thought this through. She wanted to remind me that we weren't talking about her taking a few days to visit her mother in Green Bay or even a week of biomedical meetings in Hawaii. (We weren't talking about baseball either, by the way.) We were talking about three months with an ocean and most of two continents between us. To go or not to go meant more than separate vacations; it amounted to a major policy decision. She wanted to say that there was still time for me to change my mind.

"We'll practice every day," I said, calmly, although my throat was dry. I watched her fold a pair of pajamas—new ones I'd never seen her wear.

"He'll need a glove, Dan," she said. She put the pajamas into the suitcase, smoothing them for a long time before she clicked the lid shut. When she looked up at me again, her brown eyes were solemn. She said, "You'd better get him a glove."

We all cried at least a little at the airport, much to the dismay of the biomedical vice-presidents and sales execs who were going to Slovenia with my wife. My daughters clung to their mother's wrinkle-resistant raincoat and wept without restraint. Jeff, in his new White Sox cap, sniffled. Madeline and I grieved more discreetly, each of us believing that the other was to blame for the pain of this parting, which carried in it, we also believed, the threat of future partings, of our choosing to be happy in worlds that failed to coincide.

*   *   *

At the first practice, the head coach lined Jeff up with all the other boys (no *girls* on the team, my daughters noticed immediately) and paired them off to play catch. At age eleven or twelve, most of the boys were five- and six-season veterans. My son had owned his glove for all of a week.

We'd spent that week trying to prepare ourselves—fielding flies and grounders, diagramming plays, thinking through the consequences. Even in the car on the way to the park, I'd kept it up. "Suppose you're in left field," I said.

"They'd never put me in *left* field, Dad," Jeff said, indicating that at least he'd learned the relative importance of various fielding positions.

"You're in left field," I repeated. "There's a runner on second and on third. Got that? Now. Let's say the batter hits a high fly ball to left field—"

"And I suppose Jeff *catches* it?" said Liz, who suspected all along that Little League stood between her and her mother in Slovenia.

"Hey," Jeff said. "What if I did? What if I *did* catch it?"

"In the *teeth* maybe," said Liz. Lauren, beside her in the back seat, giggled.

Jeff started to protest but then stopped to think. "Would that count, Dad? Would the batter be out if the fielder caught the ball with his teeth?"

It was a question I wouldn't have thought to ask when I was eleven. "I guess so," I said. "I guess the batter'd be out. Of course, so would the teeth."

"Well, what if you, like, caught it, like, between your knees?"

"Dangerous situation," I said, and Lauren giggled again. "But I'd say the batter would be out."

Now Liz was taking an interest. "What if you caught it in your shirt?" she said. "If you made like a net with your shirt and caught it that way? Would that count, Daddy? Would the batter be out?"

"I don't know—oh, I suppose so. As long as your *person* keeps the ball from hitting the ground, the batter's out." I hoped that would be the end of it.

"Okay," said Jeff slyly, picking up his new glove from the seat between us and tracing the stitching with his thumb, "but what if the ball was going so fast it went right *into* the fielder and got stuck in him?"

"Gross," said Lauren.

Jesus, I thought.

"Would the batter be out, Dad?"

I decided to be matter-of-fact. "The batter would be out," I said.

"Would they call the game then? If somebody hit a line drive and killed an outfielder?"

"I'm sure they would," I said, "but I don't think any kid in this league could—"

"Would the batter's team forfeit?"

"Look," I said. By now my palms were sweaty on the wheel and I was glad to see the park entrance ahead. "I doubt if the rule book covers death in the outfield—which never happens anyway—and I don't want to talk about this anymore." As we made the turn into the park, I already had the sinking feeling that I'd made a big mistake, perhaps several. We got out of the car and walked toward a knot of boys untangling into two long lines in the open field beyond the parking lot. "I bet they *would* have to forfeit," Liz said just before we reached them.

"I don't know," Jeff mused as he walked away from us, backwards, to join the boys. "What if the umpire didn't see it?"

I spent the first practice alone, the girls having deserted me for the sandbox. Watching my son lob and chase the ball for half an hour, I tried to draw it into his glove at least once in a while by the force of my concentration alone, thinking things like, Charge it, Jeff! Step into it! While I watched, memories I'd held off until now elbowed their way into consciousness—memories of lobbing and chasing my way through a Little League season twenty-five years ago, of flinching from fastballs at the plate, of finding out that I wasn't good enough, in spite of what my mother'd always told me. I remembered how much it had hurt me to learn that. And now, sitting on the grass in the treacherous May sunshine, pretending to listen as Jeff's coach explained the logical connection between uniforms and candy sales, surrounded by Little League parents, of whom I was one, I felt for the first time the full weight of having let my son in for the same lesson.

But that wasn't all. As the father—I suddenly realized—I was going to have to go through it all again, too. Not just the fielding errors and the flinching, but the whole terrible business of growing up—the unrelievable restlessness and irretrievable loss, the loneliness and vulnerability of innocence just beginning to crumble—all that grief I'd thought was behind me suddenly lay ahead of me again. All that grief times *three*. Madeline, if she had been there, probably would have smiled at my sudden insight, but she, we know, was an ocean and most of two continents away. I was alone with it, and stunned.

I stood up, thinking of escape, and took a giant step past the parents beside me to the edge of the group. From there I shielded my eyes to look for my daughters—my *little* girls—in the sandbox on the far side of the field. I spotted Lauren flat on her back in the sand, flapping her arms to make an angel. She seemed safe enough—calm, unsuspecting, oblivious enough. Lizzie, on the other hand, was sitting off to the side, watching the sand sift through her fingers. At seven and a half, she already looked a little too pensive for me. And what about Jeff? He was still out there with the other boys, looking precariously taller and thinner than I'd ever seen him before, with that new glove on the end of his arm like a growth. I felt a sudden urge to dash across the field and rescue him, shielding my head from flying baseballs, running the gauntlet to save my boy, to take him home where his frog was waiting for flies and june bugs and couldn't care less if he could catch a *ball* or not.

Instead, I sat down again on the grass. Up front, the coach had gotten as far as distributing the fund-raising candy, checking off names on a clipboard as his assistant handed out twenty-count cartons of chocolate bars. When he called my son's name, I raised my hand to accept my share.

*   *   *

I didn't write to Madeline right away. Her mailing address changed every couple of days at first, and I didn't like the idea of my letters lying abandoned in one foreign post office after another. Left behind.

Two games into regular season play—nearly a month after the first practice—Madeline finally sent us her "permanent" address for the summer, and, although I didn't much like the sound of that, I sat down to write the first long letter I'd ever had occasion to write to her in thirteen years of marriage. Most of it was about baseball.

I was as honest as I knew how to be. I didn't try to hide the fact that we lost the opener twenty-four to zip. (After four innings of walking Yankee batters home, they finally called the game in accordance with Little League rules regarding hopeless cases.) I told her pitching was not our strong suit. I told her Jeff struck out once and walked twice in the first game and got a base hit in the second, but died on third every time. I even admitted that he got hit square in the back once by a wild pitch, but he wasn't hurt, he was fine. I didn't tell her how he dropped the bat and arched his back when the ball hit him, or how visions of Jeff in traction, of my son paralyzed for life, had flashed through my mind in the long seconds before he turned slowly and walked to first base, where he stood, fighting tears. Maddie, I wrote instead, you should see your son crouching in right field with his hands on his knees, waiting for the swing, looking for all the world like a baseball player. I can tell which one is Jeff because his jersey says Number 9, but sometimes I have to scan the field and wonder, Where's my boy?

It was a good letter. In the end, I told her that we all missed her (especially me), that a box turtle had followed Lauren home from kindergarten, and that my peach blossoms had set and left us with a bumper crop of green baby peaches. Then I put my letter, along with Lauren's drawing of the turtle, Lizzie's painstaking page and a half that I had to swear not to read because it was private, and Jeff's three-line note, into an envelope. It was hard to seal it—that seemed too final, like closing the door on someone, or hanging up the telephone—so I left it open in my shirt pocket while we walked down to the post office, where we made copies, in case the letter got lost in the mail. It had a long way to go, after all.

The very next day ("By magic!" Lizzie said; "Or ESP," said Jeff), we got our first full-length letter from Madeline. We'd had daily postcards that arrived in clumps and some phone calls (most with such bad connections that Lauren came away from her turn convinced that Lizzie must be right when she said that Mom would forget how to speak English) but this was a big fat envelope with separate envelopes for each of us inside, and pictures. There was one of Madeline smiling beside a little black car with an orchard full of flowering trees behind her. ("Peaches!" the back of the picture said.) The one Lauren found most promising showed Madeline standing in some blue, blue water, with clustered stone houses and a steeple rising on the rocky shore behind her. It must have been taken from a boat or a pier. She was lined up with three of her grinning biomedical compatriots and three unsmiling Slavs, one of whom (the one next to Madeline) looked like Omar Sharif. They all had their shoes off and, where necessary, their pant legs rolled up.

"Look—Mom's swimming in Slovenia!" Lauren said.

Late that night, after the children were in bed, I considered the beach shot again over a can of beer at the kitchen table. I flipped it over and read, "Piran," in Madeline's up-and-down hand. "100 km from Ljubljana, 50 km south of Trieste." Then, in sly parentheses, "On the Adriatic Sea."

"I know that," I said out loud to the picture. "I know that Slovenia is on the Adriatic Sea."

But I didn't know it.

"Hey, Dad," somebody said, and I jumped.

Jeff was in the kitchen doorway, in the torn shorts and T-shirt he wears for pajamas. "I forgot about this," he said, holding up the jar he uses to catch his frog's dinner. I nodded. He squinted at the jar in the air in front of his nose for a moment as if he expected, instead of emptiness, a spontaneous generation of june bugs. Then he lowered it and looked at me. "Dad," he said. "You know what?"

"What?"

"You know Mick?—he's on first?—he asked if I'd help him catch a frog down in the lower park. After a game maybe."

Mick is barely four feet tall and he cries every time he strikes out, but he can field a ball like nobody's business.

"Sure," I said. "Why not?"

"Maybe tomorrow?"

"Tomorrow's fine."

Jeff stayed where he was, in the doorway, rolling the jar between his palms. After a moment or two of my waiting for it to slip and shatter around his bare feet, he said, "Who were you talking to?"

"Me?" I said. He nodded. "Just now, you mean?" He nodded again. I was casual. "Oh, nobody really. Myself, I guess."

"Oh," he said. I thought he'd go then, but he stayed, hugging the jar to his chest. "You know," he said, "I told Lizzie she was crazy, what she said about Mom. People don't forget to speak English that fast."

"No," I said.

"I mean, it's like riding a bike. You never forget a thing like that."

"No," I said, "you never forget."

He disappeared into the back hall shadows then. The screen door squeaked. I looked again at the snapshot of Omar and friends on the beach. I thought, my wife is ankle-deep in the Adriatic Sea, and I'm not even sure if the water sloshing around her toes is sweet or salt.

*   *   *

Divorce, I soon learned, was rampant in our little corner of the Little League. A lot of White Sox—including our tearful first baseman Mick—alternated parents on a weekly basis during the summer, and we lost our best pitcher (the only one capable of throwing a strike) to a custody dispute in Des Moines. I heard more than one father complain that at least they could have waited until the season was over.

And then there was Timmy the catcher's mother, who got so excited that she knocked her lawn chair over backwards jumping up to scream, "Hurry! Hurry! Hurry!" during a textbook-perfect slide that my son accidentally executed—on a pop fly the shortstop dropped—in the last inning of the first game the White Sox won that season. (Accidental or not, it was a beautiful thing to see, I wrote Madeline, a graceful glide home.) The catcher's mother ran over to Jeff as he came off the field and gave him a high five while a slow, sweet grin of amazement spread across his dusty face. Apparently, they knew each other.

"That's Timmy's mother. She helps at practice sometimes," Jeff told me. "Her name's Jean."

I knew her from observation only as a woman who came to the games dressed to the teeth in designer sportswear or flouncy sundresses and sat with her neighborhood support group in lawn chairs on the first base side, while a guy who was obviously her estranged husband—a pest exterminator from the look of his truck—hunched on the ground behind the dugout or played catch with their son, all the while stealing glances at her across the bleachers. To tell the truth, I wrote Madeline, they both steal glances at each other across the bleachers.

But there were plenty of things I did not tell Madeline about the catcher's mother. I never mentioned how long and tan her legs were, or how she struck up a conversation with me after the Perfect

Slide by asking what language my daughters were speaking under the bleachers, or how we got to talking, she and I, first about Slovenia and what my wife was doing there—"Is it *safe* to travel there?" she asked; I told her I hoped so—and then about Little League—"This is your son's *first* season? How *brave* of him!"—and then, after moving quickly through the weather, gardening, and peaches (her favorite fruit), about the difficulties of being a single parent—"even *temporarily*," she said. I also left out of my letters how she took us all out for ice cream to celebrate the slide and the ensuing victory. I surprised myself that evening by having a nice time, except for a few painful seconds walking away from the field, when I happened to glance over my shoulder and glimpse the face of a man watching his wife leave with his kid—and somebody else. I was remembering the look on his face when I went home and wrote Madeline the longest letter yet, ending it with a postscript in purple crayon: P.S. Come home soon. Without you I will surely die. Of pneumonia. From taking cold showers.

*   *   *

I'd made it halfway through the season—at home my peaches were beginning to show promise of someday growing fuzz and turning sweet—when Jeff came running to the bleachers in the top of the fifth, with the score at two and two. He was excited. "I get to play second base!" he said.

The White Sox were trying hard to maintain a two-game winning streak at the time, and all of our opponents' runs so far had been the work of a pair of lefties, one of whom was the only girl in the league and both of whom had sent the ball long and high to right field, where Jeff should have caught it. Jean, the catcher's mother, who was sitting in the bleachers that day in a denim miniskirt, had socked my arm gently the first time Jeff let the ball sail over his head and patted it in sympathy the second time, her knee pressing ever so slightly against my thigh. I avoided the eyes of the other parents.

"What about Nolan?" I asked Jeff. The regular second baseman.

"He's playing right field. Can I have a quarter for some licorice?"

It was a calculated risk the coach was taking, I thought as I dug into my pockets. Vacations and divorce settlements had left him with only enough White Sox to cover the field. Moving his weak spots around was about the best he could do. Sure enough, first pitch next inning, their first lefty—the boy—got a double off a hit that Nolan *almost* caught, recovered, and pelted to the shortstop to hold the runner at second. I heaved a sigh of relief. Our pitcher—a new and, for us, inappropriately capable boy—was so nervous with Jeff and a runner at second, that he threw the next batter three balls between strikes two and three. That made one out and one man on base when their second big hitter stepped up to the plate. The other lefty. The girl. (She reminded me of my sister, a great hitter born twenty years too early, who used to sit in the bleachers and yell at me, "Elbows up, Danny! Hey! Step into it!") As the girl tapped first one heel and then the other with the tip of her bat, I happened to catch Jeff's eye. He grinned at me and smacked his fist into his glove.

After that, things happened fast. There was the pitch, the crack of the bat, and Nolan was deep in right field, charging the ball—not the fly ball we all expected but a line drive so low I would have let it go for safety's sake. The other runner sprang brazenly off second base, leaving Jeff behind with his glove held out in front of him, probably the only person in the park who fully expected Nolan to do exactly what he did—dive for it, roll, and come up grinning, with the ball in his glove held high.

The stands erupted—lawn chairs overturned, pop spilled, babies startled into tears—and the runner, halfway to third by now, scrambled to get back. Nolan must not have heard the coach's frenzied "Shortstop! To the shortstop!" Nolan must have been on autopilot, or simply out of his head, because the next thing he did was throw the ball to second base. To Jeff. The crowd stopped, aghast, in midscream.

Then a miracle occurred. Without moving an inch left or right, Jeff held out his glove and the ball came right to it. He staggered back a step on impact, staring at it: a surprising egg in a brown nest. An instant later, the desperate runner crashed into him from behind. All at once, Nolan and the shortstop were pounding Jeff's back in ecstasy, the pitcher was throwing his cap in the air, and our bushy-browed coach, at first base, was looking incredulous. Jean grabbed my arm and shouted, "He caught it! He caught it!" Lauren and Lizzie even poked their heads out from under the bleachers to ask, in English, what was going on. "A double play!" Jean yelled at them.

"Wait a minute," I said, gripping her hand on my arm.

There was something wrong out on the field. The White Sox weren't retiring. The runner who'd collided with Jeff seemed to be crying, holding his stomach as if he'd taken a punch. The screaming and hugging in the stands subsided into silence as our coach strode over to the little conference developing in the vicinity of second base, where Jeff and Nolan and the sniffling runner looked at their shoes while the enemy coach pointed at my son and said angry things I couldn't quite make out. In the end, the runner returned to second base, Jeff went to right field, Nolan back to second, and the news spread to the fans: the other coach had accused Jeff of obstructing the runner, shoving him away from the base. The umpire hadn't seen it. They argued. The cords on the coach's sunburned neck stood out so far that I could see them from the bleachers, but the ump held firm, and that would have been that.

Except that Jeff confessed. Not to obstructing the runner, the way the coach said, but to something else that no one had noticed. Jeff told them he'd forgotten, in the excitement of finding the ball in his glove, that he had to tag up. He never touched the base. But he must have tagged the *guy*, right? the baffled umpire said. That depended on what you mean by *tagged*, Jeff said. He got the runner in the stomach with his elbow all right, but he never actually touched him with the ball. From the stands, we could see the umpire give our coach a helpless, hopeless look.

Three runs later, when the White Sox finally came in off the field, our coach had to grab the pitcher by the shoulder to keep him from punching my son. At some point during the rest of that inning—I must have been looking at my shoes—Jeff disappeared from the bench. In the top of the sixth, I left the girls with Jean and went looking for him.

I found him lying on his stomach by the side of the pond, eye to eye with a fat bullfrog he was holding in both hands. His white knickers were algae-green to mid-thigh, his socks and leggings in a muddy heap at the water's edge. He didn't look up when I sat down on the damp grass beside him. He said in a voice that rose and plunged dangerously, "I thought it wouldn't count if the umpire didn't see it."

"Jeff," I said. My son, my boy, my firstborn, my life all over again. "Jeff." He didn't look at me. I resorted to an old ploy he'd probably outgrown. "I want to tell you a secret."

He looked up. His eyes were hardly red, but the dirty streaks under his nose and across both cheeks gave him away. "Yeah?" he said.

"I hate baseball."

Jeff rolled his eyes and turned back to the frog. "I know *that*," he said.

"You do?" I thought about all the diagrams and practicing and spectating I had done so cheerfully. "How do you know that?"

He shrugged and sat up, clapping his baseball cap over the frog, who ribbeted in protest. "I guess you're not so great at hiding how you feel about stuff." He sniffled.

"Oh," I said. I had a fleeting, frightening thought then about my letters to Madeline, and about Jean, the catcher's mother, and whether it was true that what the umpire didn't see didn't count. I came back with, "But you don't know *why* I hate baseball. Not even your mother knows that."

"Why, then?" he said.

So I told him the story about my sister—the one who was always telling me to keep my elbows up at the plate, the one who could hit and catch and pitch the pants off any kid on the playground, only they didn't allow girls in Little League back then. I told him that she had gone to my coach behind my back and begged him to boot me off the team. I couldn't hit, I couldn't catch, I couldn't throw, she said. What was worse, I seemed maddeningly unaware that I couldn't.

Jeff interrupted. "Couldn't you, really?"

"What—hit, you mean?"

"And throw and catch?"

You'd think a boy would give his dad a break. "I guess I wasn't up to my sister's standards," I told him.

The baseball cap with the frog underneath hopped tentatively. Jeff stretched one leg out to keep it from escaping, pressing the visor into the grass with his toes. "So did the coach bump you?" he asked.

"No, he said he couldn't do it, no matter what, on principle."

"Did you know your sister talked to him?"

"Yes. She told me afterward. Said she was sorry. She couldn't help herself."

"So did you quit?"

"No. I guess I stuck it out on principle, too." I sighed, remembering.

Jeff thought about that. He curled his toes off the visor of his cap and watched it make its boldest leap yet toward the water. Then he asked, "What principle?"

It was a good question. My mind leapt to the shores of the Adriatic, where I saw Madeline on a beach, looking lonely. "I don't know what principle," I said.

The cap hopped again and Jeff had to lunge for it, plucking it off just in time for the bullfrog to splash into the pond with a throaty and triumphant croak. "I wonder if they have frogs in Slovenia," he said. I told him they probably did.

*   *   *

On the following Wednesday afternoon, while I sat under a peach tree thinking about Madeline and Omar and friends, Jeff surprised me by coming out on the porch in full uniform, with his glove under his arm. I thought we were through with baseball, but he said, "I'm ready to go," and thundered down the wooden steps to the driveway. At the park, our new pitcher turned his back when he saw us coming, but the catcher's mother waved from her lawn chair, Nolan said, "Hi, Jeff," and little Mick (who's on first, remember) gravely nodded hello. Jeff got a hit in the fourth inning—his second of the season—but died on third as usual. After the game, he took Mick and Nolan down to the pond and caught a frog for each of them. We were in the car, halfway home, before he told us that he'd quit the team.

"You quit?" I said, glancing over at him. He was grinning in the passenger seat. "What did you tell the coach?"

"I told him," he said, "that we might be going a-broad." Jeff, in his crumbling innocence, finds this expression amusing.

Lauren leaned forward hopefully from the back seat. "Does that mean we can go swimming with Mom in Slovenia?"

"Wait a minute," I said. "What about my peaches?"

"You could take some with you," said Liz, so quickly that I knew they had all been giving the matter some thought. I pictured myself packing hard, green peaches among my socks and underwear.

"I don't know," Jeff was saying. "Would American fruit ripen on a windowsill in, like—" he hesitated, and Liz finished for him, "Ljubljana?"

I told them it probably would.

The Dress from Bangladesh

At first Joan felt only twinges—a quickening of the pulse as she reached for a can of coffee, a pang of guilt in the vicinity of bananas. Twice, in the weeks since she'd bought the dress, she had come home from the supermarket unable to explain to Charlie and the girls why she purchased nothing but a twenty-five-pound bag of rice or a gnarled ginger root as big as her hand. Today she got a cart, rolled it through the automatic doors, and turned right, through the Seasonal and Impulse items—Velcro can holders, ice cube trays—to Fresh Produce, where, swept along by vegetable abundance, she gathered snow peas and mushrooms, bean sprouts and water chestnuts, perhaps a dozen other yellow, red, and leafy vegetables, and a hefty chunk of tofu. She didn't know that she was shopping to satisfy a hunger as big as the world. She grabbed a ten-pound bag of Idahos with one hand and with the other an unseasonable sack of yams, hoisting them both into the cart with some difficulty. On top of these went the fruit, freshly doused by the automatic sprinkling system: waxed apples, seedless grapes, peaches, pears, plums, pomegranates, canteloupe, kiwi, and bananas.

The bananas were on special—twenty-nine cents a pound. They were a product of Honduras, according to the boxes lined up on the floor around the banana bin. Joan stopped, dangerously as it turned out, to consider. Honduras was far away. Somewhere—she pictured the map—south of Mexico. How could they ship a pound of bananas from Honduras to Econofoods for only twenty-nine cents? she wondered. It cost more than that to mail a one-ounce letter from Davenport to Des Moines.

Product of Honduras, the boxes said.

Not very accurately, Joan imagined bare-chested Hondurans shinnying up the trunks of trees and slicing off great bundles of bananas like the ones she had seen from time to time in *National Geographic*. Skinny boys, glistening and vulnerable, reached up to catch the bananas their brothers cut from the trees. Bent double under their burdens, they padded flat-footed over sharp-bladed leaves to where a fat white man in a safari hat minded the scales. Joan felt the tropical heat searing the skin of the young men. She felt the steamy air fill their lungs. She saw their muscles strain, their knees buckle.

Joan put back the bananas.

But other aisles presented other problems. Reaching for a bag to fill with Fresh Roast Colombian in Aisle Two, she saw brown children picking coffee beans with delicate fingers; in Aisle Seven, it was black men, thin and hungry and hatless in the sun, hacking at sugar cane. In Meat and Seafood, she found her sympathies extended to other species. She pictured plump chickens trapped in tiny cages. She gazed in horror at the tank where hungry lobsters picked at one another, their great claws rubber-banded or torn or missing. Behind the meat counter, where other shoppers saw only the butcher turning out plastic-wrapped packs of beef, Joan saw cattle ankle-deep in mud and misery, she heard them lowing as they awaited their turn on the killing floor.

The huge hunger that had made Joan load her cart to overflowing left her. Now she felt a little ill. She pushed her fruits and vegetables toward the checkout, growing weaker and colder, shakier and dizzier, with every step, until, only yards from the No Candy lane, she felt so weak that she could no longer push the cart, and she abandoned it, fleeing through a supermarket scene that kept receding and advancing all around her like a film going in and out of focus. Amid the general roar of blood and static in her ears she heard someone shouting, "Hey! Lady! What about your groceries?"

In the car she sat very still, keenly aware of the rolled-up windows and the hard blue sky outside, the heat crowding up against her skin. Her hands lay heavily in her lap, pressing cotton fabric still cool from the supermarket air against her thighs. She was wearing the dress from Bangladesh.

*   *   *

Joan Danchek was not some kind of flake. She wasn't even an activist, although she did her share of community service. Two-term president of the PTA at the elementary school and secretary of Home and School at the junior high, she also served on two volunteer boards—Public Library and Friends of Art—and had coached fifth-grade soccer. In her only brush with the issues of her day, she had collected signatures for the local Save-the-Earth consortium in their campaign to mandate recycling in her subdivision, and later had her kitchen remodeled to accommodate the large bins for sorting plastic, paper, metal, and glass.

She had stopped at Kmart with the girls to pick up a roll of film on the way home from school, when she spotted the dress on a sale rack. Joan was not in the habit of buying her clothes at Kmart, but this was a light, loose, V-necked, double-breasted jumper in the kind of cotton plaid she used to wear in grade school. There was only one left. She checked the label. One hundred percent cotton, it said. Machine wash cold, line dry. One size fits all. Made in Bangladesh. Joan called to Kate, who was showing Lita how to juggle little boxes of panty hose.

"Look at this, Kate." Joan held up the dress for Kate to see.

"Mom, we didn't come here to go shopping."

"But it's only $9.99!" Joan said. "You can hardly go wrong for $9.99."

In the fitting room, with Kate scrunched in the corner reading a magazine and Lita hopping on one foot just outside the curtain, Joan lifted her arms over her head and entered the dress from Bangladesh like a diver parting water. The fabric fell, soft and cool, over her shoulders. It slid past her bare arms, skimmed her hips, and came to rest, the hem brushing her calves. She smoothed the skirt—it was very fine, lightweight cotton, almost translucent. Joan did a fair amount of sewing herself, when she wasn't typing up minutes or managing library book sales. The dresses she made for her daughters were, she'd always thought, a kind of vicarious caress, a way of holding the girls, if not in her arms then at least in what her hands had made—and she always paid attention to details of construction, admiring things like double rows of topstitching and lined pockets. The dress from Bangladesh had both. Joan pictured a brown-skinned woman in a sari, her bare feet rocking the treadle of an ancient sewing machine, her shoulders hunched over the work, nimble fingers smoothing a seam, or holding the plaid straight and steady under the needle. Did women wear saris in Bangladesh? Joan wondered as she slipped her hands into the nicely lined pockets on the front of the skirt.

She withdrew them at once, as if she'd been stung.

She had felt something. Inside the pockets.

Cautiously, with the very tips of her thumb and forefinger, Joan pulled the pockets away from the skirt and peered inside, half-expecting a scorpion or a tarantula or whatever ghastly vermin might make its way around the world in the pocket of a plaid dress from Bangladesh. There was nothing, not even lint. She rubbed her palms against her thighs—and stopped. She'd felt it again, more subtle this time but still distinct, a vibration, an electric tingle, as if a current moved from the dress into her skin and through it, into the muscle, and deeper, all the way to the bone, where it lodged, a dull ache. She frowned, rubbing her thigh, but the ache remained.

In the corner of the fitting room, Kate looked up from her magazine and asked, "What's the matter?"

"I felt something," said Joan.

Kate closed the magazine and stretched. "Can we go pretty soon, Mom? I'm hungry."

"Me, too!" Lita cried, poking her head through the curtains into the fitting room. "I'm *starving*."

"Okay, okay," said Joan. She pulled the dress off slowly. It tingled faintly when she draped over her arm.

*   *   *

The following week, on a hot afternoon in June, Joan wore the dress to a Friends of the Library meeting and, while the tingle and ache she'd felt in the fitting room did not return, she found herself plagued by a terrible restlessness. Barely able to sit through the meeting, she sought relief afterward by wandering through Reference and Periodicals, looking up facts on Bangladesh.

"Did you know," she asked her daughters when she got home, "that eighty-six percent of the people in Bangladesh live below the poverty level?"

The girls were on the couch, reading. Lita did not emerge from her Nancy Drew book, but Kate looked up. "That's terrible," she said.

Joan added, "They can't even afford a nutritionally adequate diet. Eighty-six percent!"

"Those poor people," Kate said, and she waited a decent interval before returning to her book.

Joan skipped the next meeting of the Friends of the Library entirely. This time she found references in the *New York Times Index* to a cyclone that had devastated Bangladesh the previous spring— half a million people dead or missing, the *Times* reported; a twenty-five-foot tidal wave had pushed fifteen miles inland and then rolled back out to sea, taking people and houses and animals with it. Sitting at the microfilm machine, Joan thought about the woman who made the double rows of perfect buttonholes on the dress from Bangladesh. Did her sewing machine lie rusting now on the floor of the Bay of Bengal?

"There were pictures in the paper," she told Charlie and the girls in the backyard when she got home. "In Bangladesh, when a cyclone comes, people tie their children to trees so they won't blow away. But this one was so bad it pulled up the trees, children and all." In the library Joan had heard the terrible ripping sound, the wailing of babies lost in the roar of the wind.

"Why don't they go in the basement?" Lita asked.

"They don't have basements, dummy," said Kate.

"It just makes you wonder," Charlie said. He was basting chicken on the grill. "Why do people insist on living in places that are clearly unsuitable for human habitation?"

Joan had no answer for that. She was still a little dizzy from watching the *Times* speed by on microfilm. The dress from Bangladesh hung heavily from her shoulders, pressing her into a lawn chair under the oak tree. Joan considered this tree. She laid a hand, fingers spread slightly, against its trunk, and looked up through the leaves to the sky.

138

*   *   *

Across the street from the Racquet Club, where Kate and Lita had swimming lessons on Saturday mornings, Joan discovered a little import store she had never noticed before she bought the dress from Bangladesh. Each week, while the girls improved their crawl stroke and practiced water safety, Joan stocked up on hand-made paper, cane baskets, jute bags, and textiles, all imported from the kinds of places newspapers identify on little maps next to stories about famine, earthquake, pestilence, and war. One morn-ing, as she lifted a tangle of jute plant hangers from a woven ham-per in the corner of the store, a voice behind her said, "They are called *sikas*."

Joan turned around. Instead of the usual Mennonite lady, a woman dressed in a sari and veil stood beside the cash register, her long brown fingers folded on the counter in front of her. "In Bangladesh," the woman said, "the people hang them from the ceil-ing and put everything inside. They are like," she hesitated, looking for a word, "like the cupboards."

"Really," Joan said. "You know, my dress was made in Bangla-desh, too." She held the skirt out in a half-curtsey.

The woman looked Joan's plaid jumper up and down. Smiling faintly, she said, "You should shop here. We buy direct."

Joan bought a bag full of jute baskets that morning and took them home, where she hung a half-dozen from the kitchen ceiling, filling them with silverware, bills, rolled-up napkins, pot holders, and bags of recyclable plastic that she took from her remodeled cupboards and drawers. In the living room, she filled four more with CDs and tapes.

"They're *sikas*," she told Charlie when he came home.

He peered into one of them and frowned. "Look like plant hangers to me."

*　　*　　*

Weeks passed. By now, Joan had owned the dress from Bangladesh for more than a month. When she wore it, she grew gaunt. She often had a haunted look, and she cooked strange things for supper from a book called *Third World Recipes* that she bought at the import store.

"Third World recipes?" said Charlie. "I thought the whole point was that they didn't *have* any food."

He and the girls dragged their forks through the caramel-colored paste on their plates for a long time one night before he finally said, "Look, Joan, I know I'm being ethnocentric and all that, but I really don't think I can eat this."

Joan was indignant. She had been pleased to find a dish that called for plenty of ginger root. "Why not?" she said. "It's rice. You like rice."

"Yeah," said Kate, "but what's this brown goo all over it?"

"That's *sauce*," Joan said. "Just regular ginger and cardamom sauce, that's all."

Some nights, they all went to bed hungry.

*　　*　　*

At the library, where she would eventually be asked to relinquish her seat on the Board of Friends, Joan filled a whole notebook with facts about Bangladesh, and when she ran out of those, she started looking up other countries—Sri Lanka, Ethiopia, Guatemala, Peru—whose names appeared on labels at the import store. The more she read about these places, the more thoughtless the people around her seemed. A mother in the park whose baby dozed in his upholstered stroller, shielded from sunlight and hunger, a pacifier lax in his mouth, seemed to her somehow worthy of reproach. There was another incident at the supermarket. Neither Joan nor the management could say exactly how it happened, and while there was at least one shopper who claimed to see the lady in the plaid dress ram her cart at full speed into the banana display, there were others who thought they saw her simply examining the fruit, like any other shopper, seconds before the crash. There was no question, the store manager said, of filing charges. The police officer was polite, even solicitous, although he did insist on calling Charlie instead of letting Joan drive home on her own.

"It was an accident," she said in the car.

*   *   *

"I can't stop thinking of things," she told her friend Mary when they met for Tuesday lunch at the All-American Deli. Joan ran her hand up and down the middle of her T-shirt, where the double row of buttons would be on the dress from Bangladesh.

"What things?" Mary looked robust and pink-cheeked, as usual. She had come from playing tennis.

"Suffering, poverty, injustice." Joan paused. "And natural disasters. Did you know, for example, that they had another big earthquake in Guatemala? Whole towns wiped out?"

"No, I didn't."

"The lady at the import store told me when I bought my bag."

"That big drawstring with the gorgeous parrot on it?"

"It's a quetzal, not a parrot," Joan said.

The last time she'd gone to the import store there had been a new clerk, a tiny woman in a brilliantly embroidered blouse and a long wrap skirt tied at the waist with a woven belt. "This," the woman had said, running her fingers lightly over the needlework on the bag Joan was considering, "is the quetzal. It is a bird sacred to the Maya people of Guatemala."

"Like the ones on your blouse?" Joan had said.

The woman tossed her waist-length braid over her shoulder and looked down at two birds perched amid blue and yellow and bright pink flowers on the front of her blouse. "Ah, no," she said. "On my *huipil* are hummingbirds. They show the triumph of love over pain and jealousy."

In the deli, Joan leaned toward her friend. She lowered her voice. "Mary," she said, "when I carry that bag, I can feel—everything. The terror. The confusion. I hear people weeping. I see houses falling in, and churches. Children crushed. If I stand very still, holding that bag, I can feel the ground shaking under my feet." Joan stopped; she hadn't meant to say so much.

Mary chewed her tenderloin thoughtfully. "Maybe you should see a shrink," she said.

Joan sat back, frowning. "I can't do that."

"Why not?"

"Charlie and the kids would think I was crazy."

*   *   *

They were already concerned. After the second incident at the supermarket, Charlie had devised a plan whereby the girls escorted Joan on shopping trips, Lita steering her clear of the dangerous aisles, while Kate darted back and forth to fill the cart. Keeping up with Lita's steady stream of conversation, Joan was not supposed to notice the growing heap of objectionable goods hidden beneath an innocent layer of bread and cereal boxes.

Kate was also dispatched to investigate the import store. Using a skinned knee as her excuse, she skipped swimming one Saturday morning and went with Joan instead. At first, Kate scoured the shop like a detective looking for clues, following Joan around and scrutinizing every item that seemed to catch her mother's eye, but soon she was finding her own objects of delight, exclaiming over clever soapstone figurines from India, holding up little leather bags from Brazil and crocheted dolls from Mexico for Joan to see. Not until the clerk—a gray-haired Mennonite lady—went into the back room to look for an undamaged pair of tiny jade elephants, did Kate remember her mission. "So where's the lady in the sari?" she whispered pointedly to her mother.

Joan looked up from a rack of handmade greeting cards. "I don't know," she said. "In the back room maybe. Sewing something."

But she wasn't. Kate asked. The clerk had never heard of a woman in a sari. Joan asked about the woman with the long black braid. The Mennonite lady had never seen her either. "But you know, dear," she said, "we're all volunteers. Some of us work only a couple of hours a week. There must be plenty of people working here that I don't know about."

"Of course," said Joan, giving Kate a look that said *so there*.

The lady went on. "If they don't work on Saturday morning,

then I wouldn't ever see them."

"I think I'll take this *sika*," Joan said quickly.

"You'll take what, dear?"

"This." Joan pushed a pile of knotted jute across the counter.

Kate placed herself squarely in front of the clerk and asked, "So you work here on Saturday mornings?"

"That's right."

"*Every* Saturday morning?" Kate said.

"Sure do." The gray-haired Mennonite lady hunted under the counter for a suitable bag or box, adding in a muffled voice, "You know, I've wrapped up more of these plant hangers for your mother than I can count." She straightened up again and smiled at Joan and Kate. "Your house must be like a hanging garden."

*   *   *

The bag from Guatemala led Joan to the meeting, or, at the very least, to the poster announcing the meeting, by slipping off her shoulder right next to the kiosk outside the library. When she stopped and turned to hoist the bag up again, she was nose-to-print with a yellow flyer pinned to the cork board in such a way that she never would have noticed it had she been hurrying past. The flyer announced a meeting of the Central American Human Rights Advocacy and Earthquake Relief Group that very evening in the basement of the Unitarian church on Gilbert and Main.

"Learn how *you* can make a difference!" the flyer said.

Joan called home to say that she'd be grabbing a bite to eat downtown.

*   *   *

In August, Joan held a rummage sale to finance her upcoming trip to Central America with the Human Rights Advocacy and Earthquake Relief Group. She planned to assist disaster victims as well as accompany human rights activists and family members of the disappeared.

"You see," she told her friend Mary, who had dropped by just in time to help Joan arrange small, seldom-used appliances on a card table in the driveway, "if U.S. citizens hang around with these people, they're less likely to get kidnapped and tortured, because nobody wants to get in trouble with Uncle Sam."

"Sounds kind of dangerous," Mary said.

Joan shrugged and stuck a tag on an electric bun warmer. "So's crossing the street," she said. She reached for a popcorn popper. "But I'd appreciate it if you wouldn't say anything to Charlie and the girls. I haven't told them about it yet."

Mary looked around the yard, which was strewn with makeshift tables full of household goods. She noted a set of gleaming wrenches spread around a tabletop sign that read All Metric Sizes. On another table she recognized Charlie's heirloom collection of decoy ducks. "Where *is* Charlie?" Mary asked.

"In Des Moines," Joan said. "He'll be back on Sunday."

*   *   *

They nabbed her on the plane in Cedar Rapids, a Saturday evening flight to Houston, with connections to Guatemala City and San Salvador. She was easy to spot, in her Bangladesh dress, the colorful quetzal bag perched on her lap. (Travel light, the Human Rights Advocacy and Earthquake Relief Group had advised her. Dress comfortably.) Airport Security turned her over to Charlie, who was waiting in the terminal.

"Joan," he told her, "you need help." He had been talking to her friend Mary. "You're not in control of your life."

Joan looked at Charlie. Waiting for takeoff, she had been thinking about things like earthquakes, death squads, cyclones, and tidal waves. She had been reviewing her notes on disease, drought, famine, flood, and war. She said, "I didn't know we were supposed to be in control."

*   *   *

For the sake of Charlie and the girls, Joan agreed to seek professional help. On the advice of her therapist, she gave the Guatemala bag and the dress from Bangladesh to her friend Mary, steadfastly ignoring the tingle and pull in her fingertips as she handed them over, one by one. When she shopped, she checked labels carefully, also on the advice of the therapist, and she always bought

American. If other people in her twelve-step program for addictive personalities started coming to group with jute-paper notebooks and Guatemala bags, well, that was hardly her fault. Joan stayed away from the import store, even after her friend Mary took a volunteer job as manager there. Joan saw her friend through the storefront window one day, arranging a display of Laotian needlework. Mary was wearing the dress from Bangladesh.

As the therapist predicted, Joan's recovery was swift. Before long, she was able to frequent the supermarket without an escort, having found that she could buy bananas, sugar, meat, even boycotted products, with impunity once again. When Christmastime approached, Joan did all her shopping at the mall, which is where she found the alpaca sweater for Charlie, in a store bedecked with Stars and Stripes and eagles—as well as holly—that called itself *American Sport*. The "Made in Peru" on the label gave her pause, it's true, but when she touched the sweater and felt no electric tingle, no mountain cold, no aching belly, no fear of armed guards sweeping into the village— nothing but luxurious softness—she knew she must be cured. To be on the safe side, she had it gift-wrapped on the spot.

Charlie loved it. "I've wanted one of these for years," he said. He pulled the sweater over his head, stroked the soft wool, and then stopped.

In the glow of the lights from the Christmas tree, Joan said, "Is something wrong?"

Charlie frowned. He moved his shoulders up and down as if he had an itch. "I don't know," he said. "I felt something."

Dear Mike the Mechanic,

I am a seventy-nine-year-old widow and own and drive a 1979 Plymouth purchased in 1979.

The red light came on.

It was my husband's car. He bought it two years before he died, and I know for a fact that in those two years of him driving it the red light never came on. My husband was an automobile mechanic, too, until he retired. His health was bad by then already, but he got himself an easier job as nightwatchman at the brewery. They paid him money for just strolling around, he used to say, getting his heart exercise like the doctor said he should. He took good care of that car, changed everything right on time and wrote it all down, on account of his being an auto mechanic all those years. There wasn't anything he couldn't fix and especially cars. Before he died he told me, Bernice, that car is going to last you a lifetime. You just forget about all those foreign jobs, this here Chrysler Corporation Plymouth will last you for the rest of your life, my *word* on it, Bernice, and I don't care if you live to be a hundred. He said that to me right in the hospital. Died in his sleep instead of waking up the next morning.

So why did the red light come on?

I asked my mechanic right away and he said it could be a lot of different things. He installed a power hose. After nine miles the red light came on again so he installed a new oil pressure switch. I started home and the light came on before I could get to my driveway. My mechanic, he came with the tow truck because I didn't want to drive it with the red light on in rush hour traffic. What if something happens when I'm making a left turn? He said sometimes the computer gets programmed wrong, so this time he installed a new thermostat. Well, two days later I picked up the car and I'm driving home and guess what happened again.

What I want to know is, why does the red light still come on? It never came on when Howard was alive. He never gave the red light a *chance* to come on when he drove that car. So what's wrong with my mechanic? Can you help?

Signed,
Mrs. Howard Schultz
Milwaukee, Wis.

Dear Mike the Mechanic,

Thank you for your prompt and personal reply. I never wrote in to a magazine before, so I didn't know what to expect. It's my sister that subscribes to *Travel*, although she never goes anywhere.

I took your advice and drove the car to the local Plymouth Service Center (with the red light on and off all the way, which I didn't care for one bit), and they're checking everything else you said. They said it will take three days, and it's going to cost me a bundle because the car is not under warranty anymore even though the mileage is so low you'd think they could give me credit for that. I only drive it for shopping and to my sister's house. Usually I walk to church (only two blocks). I quit having my hair done over a year ago. It looks a lot better now (my sister gives me a home permanent and I give her one, just like when we were young), better than it did in all those years I trotted off to have it teased and sprayed up stiff. Howard never did like it fixed like that. He told me to just leave it. You have nice hair, he said, leave it alone. But you know how it is. The ladies at the church resale shop all have their hair dyed and sprayed so I had to have it, too. The things women do to themselves, I just don't know why. Now it turns out that Howard was right all along, and my hair looks much better this way and it feels soft, not like cotton candy. Sometimes I think of Howard getting that stiff stuff instead of hair to touch and well, I can tell you it makes me feel pretty bad. You never know anything until it's too late to do you any good.

147

Sincerely,
Mrs. Howard Schultz
P.S. I get the car back on Tuesday.

Dear Mike the Mechanic,

I got the car back on Tuesday with everything new like you said. Wednesday it worked fine. I drove it to the mall and SuperFoods, no problem. Then on Thursday, on the way to my sister's which is almost the only other place I ever drive to as I said before, although I do get around more than a lot of people my age, the red light came on! I drove straight back to the Plymouth dealer instead of my sister's and he said sometimes the computer gets programmed wrong. I told him I heard that one before. Then he says it's probably a short in the circuit and he'll have the mechanics take a look at it for nothing if I can leave it overnight. I said I left it three whole days before. He says it's the best he can do. I took the bus home.

I don't know if they did anything to it or not. When I came back the next day (my sister went with me on the bus, bless her heart) the car was parked in the exact same spot where I'd left it, only three other cars were blocking it in now. It took half an hour more for them to get it out of there.

The red light stayed off for three days after that, and I was so happy I was tempted to go back and give that mechanic some cupcakes or cookies or something. Then, on the way to Shopko, it came on again. My sister was in the car, so she saw it, too. I said to her, Am I crazy? Or is there something wrong with this car?

Can you help?
Mrs. Howard Schultz
Milwaukee, Wis.

Dear Mike the Mechanic,

Last night somebody broke into my garage! I think it was kids, because they left beer cans and one of them (excuse me to say it) moved their bowels on the hood of my car.

Can you believe it? Why anyone would do such a thing is what I can't understand. And why me, my car? I called the police and they were willing to stand around with their belts and holsters creaking and write everything down but when they went out to the garage they wouldn't clean the car off. I had to hose it down myself.

Whoever it was took my electric lawn mower (which makes me think maybe it was one of the boys I had cut my grass last summer) and all of Howard's wrenches. Every last one, American and metric. Also his tachometer, and a pipe cutter (Howard always did all our own plumbing repairs and also my sister's since her husband passed away) and an air compressor he built himself and the battery charger. All of it gone. Now what is my son-in-law going to use when he comes over to change his oil and things like that? I suppose he'll go somewhere else to do it now and I'll *never* get to see my grandchildren anymore. (My daughter teaches at the university and is too busy for all normal purposes.)

I can't understand what makes people do things like this. They know when a woman is alone. Nobody *ever* broke into our garage when Howard was alive, I hope you know—even though he was weak as a kitten those last few months and I did everything for him and even cut the grass myself when Larry (that's my son-in-law) couldn't get over to do it. But nobody ever so much as cut through our yard when Howard was alive. Now I've got a regular thoroughfare here.

But I shouldn't complain. Do you know what they did to my sister's house? They shot a hole through the wall of her living room. With a real gun, a rifle. The bullet ended up stuck in her stereo, which is just as well or it might have ended up in my sister, who was sitting there watching TV at the time. Can you imagine how she felt? And now she can't listen to her records anymore either, which seems like a small thing to someone who has lots of other things to do and money to spend, but a thing like that is really important when you're alone. Sometimes the silence makes your ears buzz. I'm not kidding.

The bullet in her stereo wasn't the only thing, either. She had her tires slashed when she still had the car and her flowers uprooted—not picked, mind you, uprooted—and little trees broken off in the yard. Why do people do these terrible things? And when I backed my car out of the garage to clean it up, the red light stayed on the whole time.

I think there must be something terribly wrong. I've gotten to where I can't even get into the car without my heart beating faster, if you know what I mean. Do I have to take it to the dump? Why can't they just fix it? Why didn't those kids take the damn car for heaven's sake, instead of Howard's tools?

Mrs. H. Schultz
Milwaukee

Dear Mike Mechanic,

You aren't the first to ask why don't I move in with my sister Harriet then.

I can only say that Harriet would never in a million years move in with me. And even if she wanted to, I wouldn't let her. No sir. My sister Harriet has a stainless steel sink (Howard put it in for her) that doesn't know what it's like to hold a dirty dish. The books on her shelves are in alphabetical order. You take one off to look at it and she's right behind you putting it back. She dries out her bathtub with a towel, *then* she dries herself.

Besides, she has this medical problem, can't hold her water too well. So she has to get up three or four times a night. Now I'm a very light sleeper—always have been, at least ever since there was a baby to listen for and how long ago was that?—and Harriet is not the kind of person who can leave a toilet unflushed.

Yours truly,
Mrs. B. Schultz

Dear Mike the Mechanic,

Life isn't fair, and I'll tell you why.

For a week I left my garage door open. Not open all the way

because then my neighbor across the alley would call me up to tell me I left my garage door open—no, just a little crack that some bunch of rowdy kids going down the alley would notice because they try all the locks.

I'm ashamed to say it, but I also left my keys in the ignition, you know, as if I forgot them. For a whole week I left them like that. A whole week I had to lay in bed at night and think about the way Howard promised me that Plymouth would last me a lifetime and now look what I was doing. I hardly slept a wink for a whole week.

On the eighth day, I could hardly believe it—they finally stole the car. I guess some nights they roam different alleys. I don't know if it was the same boys as before, but you should have heard them go on about what a stupid old biddy I was to go and leave my keys for them. I swear, some of them didn't sound any older than my grandson Larry, Jr., and he's only thirteen. They didn't even push the car out and roll it down the alley a ways so nobody'd hear. They just started it up and backed it out as bold as you please. And there I was upstairs listening and feeling guilty about Howard's car and wishing they'd drive away quick so I could forget I'd heard anything, so it wouldn't be so hard to be surprised when Marianne (my neighbor across the way) called me in the morning, all excited, to say she just looked out her kitchen window and did I know that I'd left my garage door open and by the way, my car was gone?

My phone rang bright and early the next morning all right, but it wasn't Marianne. It was a nice, very polite young police officer who made my acquaintance on a previous occasion, and he was so pleased because I would be happy to learn that five juveniles had been apprehended the night before at the end of my alley as they perpetrated a grand theft auto, and the stolen property had been duly recovered. I was lucky, the officer said, that they got caught before they had a chance to strip it down or take it for a joy ride which is what they usually do. Now all I had to do was come down to the station house to get my car back. Oh, and he just wanted to mention that one of the arresting officers who drove the car back to the station happened to notice that the red light was on, so perhaps I should have that looked into.

I was so upset I thought about leaving the car right there at the police station, but my sister Harriet (who does *not*, by the way, know exactly *why* I was so upset) says, well, maybe there was some larger design at work here—what with Howard saying what he did about the car practically on his deathbed—and I shouldn't mess it up. When Harriet was a Catholic, everything was God's will. We heard so much about God's will at Howard's funeral, as I recall, that I started to think maybe it was a little disrespectful of Howard to hang on as long as he did. Now that she's a Unitarian, it's always some larger design that makes everything happen. I told her maybe it was just rotten luck, but we went down on the bus to get the car. We were waiting on a bench for the paperwork to be done, when an officer came out of a door with two boys and set them on another bench across the hall with handcuffs on. One of them *was* the boy who cut my grass last summer and I'll say this for him—at least he hung his head in shame. The other boy said something rude and threatening to Harriet and me, and the red light stayed on all the way home.

I feel terrible. Harriet says things could be worse, but I don't see how.

Sincerely,
Bernice M. Schultz

Dear Mike,

Don't be alarmed! Please excuse the hospital stationery. (Such short sheets—ha!) Harriet is in the bed next to mine with a slight concussion of the brain because the nurses wanted to keep us together. I am fine under observation with only a sprained wrist, and I don't ever have to worry about the red light again. But here comes a Pink Lady with lunch.

More to come,
B. Schultz 1009A

Dear Mike the Mechanic,

Such nice flowers by wire, you shouldn't have! Harriet and I are a little famous around here by now. (You can keep the clippings. I have copies.) I don't suppose you get the Channel 12 Action Reporter on TV where you are, but he's the one who got us on the waiting list for a high-rise apartment with guards and elevators just for older people like ourselves. (The hospital put Harriet on medication for her water problem that's done wonders, by the way, although of course they didn't mention that on TV.) Some viewers even sent contributions, mind you—money and canned goods—not just for my sister and me but for the families of the boys who are all in some halfway kind of rehabilitation, except for the little guy in his mother's custody. I don't know what Harriet and I will do with so much soup and fruit cocktail, but it's the thought that counts.

In response to your question, here is what happened, if you believe it or not.

After we picked up the car from the police last week Monday, my sister insisted on spending the night, seeing as I was so upset. Now it was perfectly clear to me that *Harriet* was scared to be by herself (she moved in for two days when they shot the hole in her stereo, two days being as much as either of us could stand) and that what I needed was a good night's sleep without kids in my garage *or* Harriet flushing the toilet, but I said how nice of her to offer. What else could I say?

Being nervous, we didn't sleep much, either of us, and when we woke up next morning we decided to take the bus to 6:30 Mass at Our Lady Queen of Sorrows, which is where we used to belong years ago before *that* neighborhood went to pot, and we still like to go there now and again for old time's sake. We waited until it was light out and then we got ready, figuring we'd beat the rush hour and avoid guitar Mass which is never that early in the morning. So there we were, waiting for the Number 62 on 16th and Mineral, in front of the bakery, when Harriet points to a car coming toward us up the wrong side of the street and says, "My, doesn't that car look like your Plymouth."

The words were no sooner out of her mouth than we both realized that of course it *was* my Plymouth.

Poor Harriet said, "Dear God," and I myself suddenly got a bad feeling in my stomach area. We turned away from the curb and pretended we were looking at something way down on Mineral Street, shading our eyes and pointing and everything. But the Plymouth pulled up to the curb anyway and a boy yelled out the window, "Hey, Gramma! You want a ride?" Harriet and I tried to walk away as if they couldn't really be talking to us. (We also looked around for help, but do I have to tell you there was nobody in sight? And Harriet, bless her heart, didn't say a word, but all the time I'm thinking that she's thinking that she *told* me we should have walked four extra blocks up to Greenfield Avenue, which is a much busier corner.)

They finally made us get into the car by two of them jumping out, grabbing Harriet and me by the arms, and pushing us into my very own back seat with one boy on either side of us against the doors. (I guess that was to make sure we would not try to leap out of a moving vehicle!) My whole car stunk from beer and who knows what else. There were five boys all together and none of them was the neighbor boy who used to cut my grass, but I did recognize the other boy from the police station. I don't know why they let him go right away, but now he was out for revenge!

They took us for a joy ride, Mike. We turned corners with two wheels up on the curb. We ran three red lights and more stop signs than I could count. (And where are the police at 6:00 A.M.? Having coffee?) We went over railroad tracks, right in front of a train, almost getting cut in half when the barricade came down. All the time Harriet was crying and squeezing my hand, as well as the hand of the boy next to her, who looked about twelve years old and ready to throw up at any minute. The other boys seemed to be having a great time, especially in the front seat, where they were passing something back and forth, I couldn't see what.

But all of that is nothing, compared to what happened next.

We were sticking to back streets (for obvious reasons), near the junk yards and the river. Around there they still have a couple of those bridges that lift up in two pieces, like drawbridges, with a man in a little building having to bring them up and down just right so they'll fit together in the middle. When we went two-wheels around the next corner, right in front of us was one of those bridges going up! It was about a block away, with the barricades already coming down, just like at the train tracks, and we weren't stopping! In fact, the boy driving gave out a whoop and the one next to me yelled, "Pedal to the metal!" (which means, "Step on the gas!") It looked like the end, when all of a sudden, Harriet reached forward and— I don't know what put this in her head since she couldn't see the dashboard anymore than I could and afterward she could hardly remember doing it at all—she grabbed the driver's shoulder and screamed right in his ear, "The red light is on!" I guess he wasn't expecting that, because he slammed on the brakes until we nearly went right over his head through the windshield!

Only it was too late to stop. With the brakes locked for sure, my Plymouth hit that bridge sideways and skidded uphill toward the sky, which was all you could see over the top of the middle of the bridge, it was so high in the air by now, even though the little man in the control building had already stopped it and called the police, we found out later. When I opened my eyes again, everyone was slid over to one side of the car, squashing Harriet, and there wasn't a sound to be heard except for some creaking and a siren in the distance and the boy next to Harriet, who was even more squashed than she was, crying.

I can tell you we had a bad moment up there, stuck at the top of the middle of the bridge with the two right wheels over the edge and our lives hanging in the balance, so to speak. Before the firemen came, the little guy next to Harriet had passed out cold and the rest of them were begging me and Harriet and God to forgive them and they'd never steal anything again if only they got out of this alive, and so forth. One boy even vowed to become a priest. It seemed to take forever, but the firemen finally came and got us all out of the car, one by one, and helped us climb down a ladder to solid ground (except for the one boy they had to carry), before they took a chance and started to lower the bridge a little. They were trying to hook up some more cables to the car, when my poor Plymouth went over the edge.

You should have seen it. The car hung by one rear wheel for a second and then down it went, head first, like it was driving into the river on purpose. It didn't sink like a stone either. It sort of bobbed and floated, tail end up, hissing and gurgling like I never heard anything in my life. And then, just as the license plate was about to disappear under the water (and like I told my daughter, I've got plenty of witnesses for this because she didn't believe it either), a red light came on! It's true. I don't know if it was the same one or not, but you could see the red glow in the water getting dimmer and dimmer until the whole car was completely gone. The red light stayed on to the very end.

I can't tell you what that means, but I know it means something.

Harriet and I will be out of the hospital in a few days. My daughter all of a sudden offered to fix up a room for me, but I told her no, maybe I'd try apartment living for a while. What with the car insurance money and the cash contributions from concerned viewers, Harriet and I thought we might treat ourselves to a little vacation. As a matter of fact, we were looking at some old copies of your magazine in the lounge this very afternoon for ideas on where we might like to go. I'm trying to remember where that postcard was from that you sent me once. With the palm trees. Can you help?

Yours truly,

Bernice

P.S. Harriet says hello.